LAURIE PAIGE

HEARTBREAKER

Published by Silhouette Books

America's Publisher of Contemporary Romance

Special thanks and acknowledgment are given to Laurie Paige for her contribution to the LONE STAR COUNTRY CLUB series.

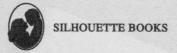 **SILHOUETTE BOOKS**

ISBN 0-373-61355-5

HEARTBREAKER

Visit Silhouette at www.eHarlequin.com

Printed in U.S.A.

Welcome to the

*Where Texas society reigns supreme—
and appearances are everything.*

Time is running out for a beloved Wainwright heiress....

Michael O'Day: This arrogant top-notch heart surgeon is impossible to ignore—especially with his piercing blue eyes. But he's about to learn a lesson in humility when he falls under the spell of his courageous patient and is faced with the moral dilemma of a lifetime....

Susan Wainwright: She refuses to let her medical crisis stop her from continuing to dazzle crowds as a star-studded ballerina. But when her pompous— potently sexy—doctor becomes personally invested in her case, she knows there is something more than ire smoldering between them. Will she place her fragile heart in his capable hands?

The Desperate Crime Lord: Dying Mob boss Carmine Mercado is hell-bent on getting his hands on a donor heart and enlisting the skills of Michael O'Day to perform the risky procedure. And he won't think twice about resorting to menace, coercion and blackmail to further his agenda....

THE FAMILIES

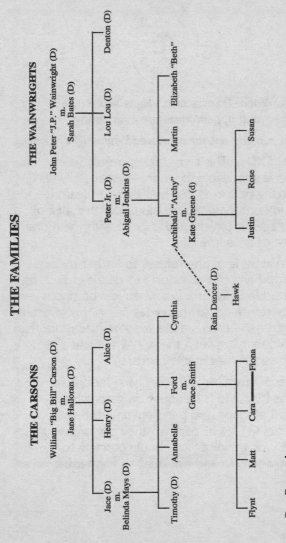

THE CARSONS

William "Big Bill" Carson (D)
m.
Jane Halloran (D)

- Jace (D)
  m.
  Belinda Mays (D)
- Henry (D)
- Alice (D)

- Timothy (D)
- Annabelle
- Ford
  m.
  Grace Smith
- Cynthia

- Flynt
- Matt
- Cara
- Fiona

THE WAINWRIGHTS

John Peter "J.P." Wainwright (D)
m.
Sarah Bates (D)

- Peter Jr. (D)
  m.
  Abigail Jenkins (D)
- Lou Lou (D)
- Denton (D)

- Archibald "Archy"
  m.
  Kate Greene (d)
- Martin
- Elizabeth "Beth"

- Justin
- Rose
- Susan

Rain Dancer (D)
- Hawk

D   Deceased
d   Divorced
m.   Married
------ Affair
■■■ Twins

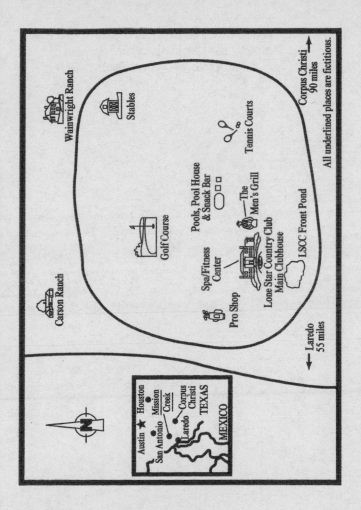

Wainwright Ranch

Stables

Tennis Courts

Golf Course

Pools, Pool House
& Snack Bar

The
Men's Grill

Spa/Fitness
Center

Carson Ranch

Pro Shop

Lone Star Country Club
Main Clubhouse

LSCC Front Pond

Corpus Christi
90 miles

All underlined places are fictitious.

Laredo
55 miles

N

Austin

Houston

Mission
Creek

San Antonio

Corpus
Christi

TEXAS

Laredo

MEXICO

This book is dedicated to Steve and Jolene Thurman:
thanks for sharing information,
experience and expertise!

One

The twin engines of Michael O'Day's new plane purred steadily as he buzzed the field in preparation for landing at Mission Ridge, a "fly in, fly out" community on the outskirts of Mission Creek, Texas. A private shuttle was off to one side, passengers filing down the plane's steps. No aircraft were on the runway, and none was heading in for a landing, other than his.

From the air, he could pick out the home he'd purchased last year. It was a big house for a bachelor, not yet completely furnished, but he was pleased with it.

With the private airstrip practically at his door and the Lone Star Country Club golf links nearby, he could indulge his two favorite pastimes: golfing and flying. He planned to retire here.

But not anytime soon. At thirty-four, he had a ways to go before riding off into the sunset. However, with the new, faster plane, it would be a piece of cake to fly the two hundred fifty miles back and forth to Houston where he had a penthouse and an office. As a heart surgeon, he kept a busy schedule.

He set the nimble four-passenger plane down on the tarmac and taxied off the runway, heading for his hangar at the back of his two-acre lot. Instead of pushing the plane inside when he arrived, he left it on the apron. He was running late for lunch with his friend and golfing buddy, Flynt Carson. He'd take care of the aircraft later.

He dashed across the back lawn, activating the remote to open the door of the garage attached to the house. Inside, he swung his legs over the car door and into the seat of the low-slung convertible he kept at Mission Ridge.

Another indulgence, he admitted, but he didn't regret the cost. The time here in the heart of Texas ranching country gave him the necessary rest and relaxation to perform his surgeries with confidence. During his internship, a wise use of one's time had been stressed, over and over by his mentor, one of the foremost cardiac surgeons in the country.

Usually Michael flew in on Friday afternoon, but he'd been delayed by emergency surgery yesterday, then had overslept this morning, making him late taking off.

Checking his watch, he grimaced and turned the ignition key. He drove out of the garage, hit the button to lower the door behind him, glanced to his left and, seeing no traffic, gunned the engine.

And immediately threw on the brakes.

The car came to a screeching halt about six inches

from a tall, lithe beauty who was standing in the middle of the street. She turned flashing green eyes on him.

"You baboon!" she said in an angry, albeit melodious voice. "You shouldn't be allowed behind the wheel, driving like a maniac down a residential street."

"Well, honey," he drawled, amused and irritated by her lofty manner, "I didn't expect some female"— translation: some ditz—"to be sashaying down the middle of the street."

"I am not 'sashaying' down the middle of the street. I happen to be crossing it."

He studied her, then glanced across the street and back to her. "You might not know it," he mentioned in a helpful, philosophical tone, "but the shortest distance between two points is a straight line. Going straight across the street gets you to the other side faster than ambling across at an oblique angle. It could also save you from getting run over."

"And watching where you're going could save you from killing someone and getting thrown in jail."

"A point well taken," he agreed, unable to kill the grin. In blue slacks and a knit top that outlined her to perfection, she was very easy on the eye. Besides which, he'd always been attracted to women with fire.

He watched her march on across the street, her

head high, her light brown hair swinging about her shoulders. He'd never seen anyone move the way she did, with the grace and dignity of a fairy princess. And the righteous anger of a tent evangelist.

A name came to him. Susan Wainwright.

He'd never met her, but he'd seen her a few times onstage. She was a lead ballerina with the Houston Ballet.

Her sister had recently wed Matt Carson. A surprising affair, considering the Carsons and Wainwrights had been feuding for nearly as long as the Hatfields and McCoys, or so he understood. But Michael recalled hearing a rumor of a truce for the wedding.

Watching the delectable sway of her hips, he formed a new appreciation for a dancer's grace of movement. To his surprise, a vision came to mind—him and her in a wide bed, long legs wrapped around him—

Whoa!

Shaking his head, he forced those thoughts aside. "Hey," he called, "you need a ride somewhere?"

Susan gave him a drop-dead glance. "No, thanks. Someone is picking me up."

A fleeting notion indicated he'd like the "someone" to be him. Forget it, he advised. That little gal was a heartbreaker from the get-go. Besides, he wasn't looking for any lengthy entanglement. His life was fine just as it was.

Grinning at himself, he eased down on the pedal and left the enticing and oh-so-haughty beauty behind.

At the Lone Star Country Club, located deep in the heart of Lone Star county, he tossed the keys to the valet and dashed inside. The Yellow Rose Café was dark compared to the bright mid-September sunshine. He paused to let his eyes adjust.

"Michael, over here," Flynt Carson called.

Michael had performed bypass surgery on Flynt's dad five years ago. He'd visited their family ranch many times since then. He and the two Carson brothers, Flynt and Matt, had become good friends.

"Hey, man, what's been happening?" Michael asked, taking a chair. A waiter hurried over with the menu and took his order for a tall glass of iced tea. "Not Texas style," he added.

Texas tea could set a man on his rump after one glass of the potent blend of liquors with a smidgen of tea and fruit flavors to round it out.

Flynt grimaced when they were alone. "I guess you heard the news about Carl Bridges?"

"Yeah, I saw it on TV. Any more info on it?"

Flynt nodded. "Spence is keeping his cards close to his chest, but they have arrested someone."

Spence Harrison was also a golfing buddy and the local district attorney handling the case.

"Anyone we know?"

"No. A member of the mob, I understand, but

don't quote me on that. It's all rumor and conjecture at present.''

''Mob'' referred to the infamous Texas Mafia that comedians loved to make jokes about, such as: Did ya hear about the Texas mafia bank robbery? When they stood back to back, their spurs got stuck. They would have gotten away, but they couldn't decide who got to ride face forward on the getaway horse. Ha-ha-ha.

Murder was never a laughing matter, Michael mused, but this case had been particularly poignant. Only days before Carl Bridges's murder, his estranged son, Dylan, had come home; days later, he'd been a suspect in the crime. Thankfully, he was cleared.

A waitress appeared—Daisy, it said on her name tag—a Texas blonde with big hair and a twang so thick it made Michael smile each time he heard her speak. He and Flynt gave their orders for the chef's Saturday luncheon special.

Movement caught Michael's attention. A lithe woman in a blue summer outfit walked into his field of vision. She was with an older woman. Her mother, he assumed, because of the similarities in their facial structure.

A ping of interest coursed through him, a tiny hum of electricity that warmed him in spite of the fan circling over their table. The two women were seated on the patio overlooking the famous golf course.

"Susan Wainwright," Flynt murmured, looking at the women, then back at Michael. "Her mother, Kate Wainwright."

"Hmm," Michael said noncommittally. The Wainwright name reminded him of another event. "How're the newlyweds?"

"Who knows? They haven't come out of their house yet," Flynt said with a straight face, then laughed.

Michael chuckled with his friend. "I was sorry to miss the wedding. I heard it was exciting."

"Yeah, but the real action was in New York, at Rose's aunt's place. It was a standoff, you might say. Justin Wainwright was threatening to shoot Matt after finding Rose had been…compromised. And I was determined to save Matt from himself. Rose's Aunt Beth distracted the warring parties while Matt and Rose slipped out and got hitched. Justin and I packed up our six-shooters and slunk home."

Michael laughed, but he knew the Carsons and Wainwrights had once been great friends. Flynt's great-grandfather had even started this very country club with his best friend and fellow rancher, J.P. Wainwright, but a falling-out over a family scandal and water rights had started a feud that had lasted three-quarters of a century.

The things people fought over, Michael reflected in disgust. If people could see the life and death struggles he saw, they'd view things differently.

No thinking about that, he chided himself. This was his fun time. However, there was one more problem to be discussed that had nothing to do with cardiac surgery in Houston. "Any word on Lena?" he asked.

The shock of his life had occurred while playing golf back in May. Right here at the posh country club, on the ninth green, in fact, the golfing foursome had found an abandoned baby. The shock had come when all four men had been suspected of being the father. Worse, they'd all admitted it was a possibility. They'd each been involved in a more or less brief liaison the previous year.

DNA testing had already proved neither Flynt, Spence nor Michael could be the sire. That left the last man of the foursome, Tyler Murdoch, to be tested.

Since Michael had been filling in for Luke Callaghan, Luke was also a possibility. The note left with the baby had gotten wet, blotting out any name of the father. The only legible part had been, "I'm your baby girl. My name is Lena."

Someone, the police had concluded, had been observing them play and had chosen the isolated ninth hole, where bushes screened a maintenance shed. Footprints indicated that someone had hidden there while watching them find the baby.

Flynt felt he needed to be the one to take care of the baby. The four of them had chipped in and hired a private investigator to find the mother or father or somebody to claim the foundling.

"I do have some other news," Flynt said, moving his hand when the waitress brought their food. "You recall we had to have Lena's DNA tested when we took her in for a thorough checkup so it could be matched to the father's?"

Michael nodded.

"They discovered she has some kind of anemia, thal—"

Daisy plopped Michael's plate down with a hard thunk. "Thalassemia," she said in a low voice.

Michael caught distress vibes from her. Reaching back to his medical school days, he came up with a stray fact. "It's a type common to those of Mediterranean descent," he explained to his friend. "Hereditary factors are definitely indicated."

"Yeah, that's what the doctor told us," Flynt said. He looked at Daisy curiously. "How did you know about the disease?"

"I got this friend," Daisy said in her brash Texas hill country accent. "She has it."

"Josie and I have been concerned about the effects on Lena's growth. Did your friend mention any particular difficulties with that?"

Flynt had hired Josie as a nanny for Lena, then ended up marrying her. Turned out, they were now expecting a little bundle of joy of their own. Fate was a funny thing, Michael thought with a silent chuckle at his friend's expense.

His gaze was drawn to the Wainwright princess while Flynt and Daisy discussed the necessary testing that should be done regularly to watch for recurrences of the anemia in baby Lena.

Susan was listening to some male friend who had stopped by her table. From what Michael could discern, the man was posturing and showing off, bragging about his hole-in-one win over some friends. She was full of congratulations, smiling as if bestowing the gold cup on the guy. Michael suppressed a jab of irritation.

What did he care whom she talked to and flirted with?

He didn't, he told himself firmly. Ah, but she was easy to look at...

"Who is that man you keep looking at?" Kate Wainwright asked. "The one sitting with Flynt Carson."

Susan jerked as if caught with her hand in the proverbial cookie jar. "No one."

"An interesting nonentity," her mother murmured. "He looks familiar. I'm sure I've seen him before."

"I don't know his name," Susan admitted, "but he nearly ran me over on the street near the airstrip.

I was on my way to the phone to give you a call and let you know I was in. We had words.''

Susan wished her mother wouldn't study the man quite so openly. She didn't want him to think they were interested in him in the least.

''Words?'' her mother inquired.

''I called him a baboon and told him he shouldn't be driving, or something like that,'' she reluctantly admitted.

Her mother looked from the man back to Susan, amusement in her eyes as if she laughed at something only she could see. Susan tried not to be irritated.

''He and his friend are leaving,'' Kate reported.

Susan deliberately turned her chair toward the golf green beyond the patio so she wouldn't have to look his way. ''Mmm,'' she said.

''Oh, he's coming over.''

Susan jerked around. Sure enough, the impolite stranger was approaching their table.

''My, he's certainly good-looking,'' Kate whispered. ''Tall. And the bluest eyes. I've always liked blue eyes with dark hair. Such a handsome contrast.''

''Mother!'' Susan whispered, reminding the other woman that the man was almost upon them.

''Hello,'' he said, stopping by their table.

She nonchalantly glanced up at him. ''The baboon.''

He laughed as if she'd said something witty, which made the heat rush to her face for some reason she couldn't fathom. Nor did he take the hostile hint to leave.

"I came over to apologize for my lack of manners when we, uh, first met," he continued. "My only excuse is that I was running late."

"Is that your usual mode of operation?" she asked coolly, ignoring the increased beat of a pulse through her temple. She pushed a wisp of hair behind her ear.

"Susan, introduce me to your friend," her mother requested, all smiles for the obnoxious man.

"We haven't formally met," he said, and held out his hand. "Michael O'Day."

Kate shook his hand. "Won't you join us?"

To Susan's further chagrin, the big ape—he was easily a couple of inches over six feet tall—pulled out a chair and sat down. "Iced tea," he said to the waiter who hurried over.

"I'm Kate Wainwright. This is my daughter, Susan."

"Flynt mentioned your names," he said in an affable manner, as if they were all the very best of friends.

His voice was deep, almost a bass, and it rushed along her nerves like one long, drawn-out note from a cello, quiet yet vibrant, as if nature itself whispered through his rich cadences.

An unexpected shudder washed over her. A faint but persistent pain pinged in her chest with each heartbeat. She pressed a hand there to still it.

"I know where I've seen you," her mother suddenly exclaimed. "I mean, besides here. There was a write-up in the Sunday paper a few weeks ago. You performed miracle surgery on the head of state from some foreign country. You're the heart specialist from Houston."

Michael bowed his head briefly in acknowledgment.

So, he wasn't falsely modest about his skill, Susan noted. He was one of the top five heart surgeons in the U.S., per her own doctor. "Bold, innovative and determined" had been said of him in the article her mother referred to.

"Susan," Kate said, a plea in the word.

Susan shook her head, warning her mother not to say anything to the arrogant heart doctor. Her own physician wanted her to go to Dr. O'Day for a consultation. So far, she'd steadfastly refused.

"Susan," her mother said, more sternly this time.

"I'll see someone," she promised.

Her mother wasn't at all deterred by her tone. "This is like…like a nudge from God. You can't ignore it."

Susan could and was determined to do so. "Don't be sil—" She broke off, unable to be rude to her mother. "I'll see a doctor soon." But not this one.

"This is a golden opportunity."

"Is there something I should know about?" the irritating doctor wanted to know.

"Susan has a heart condition," Kate answered before Susan could reply.

"Ah, I see."

Susan felt his gaze on her, as incisive as a laser beam. "It's nothing," she said, and heard the stubborn denial in her tone. "I'm fine."

"You collapsed on the stage at your last performance," her mother reminded her sternly.

"I—I was tired."

"Collapsed?" he questioned. "I've seen you perform. You were magnificent."

Amazed, she stared at him. He looked sincere. Maybe he wasn't such a baboon, after all, she conceded, since he obviously recognized her talent. She silently laughed at her own cockiness. She was as sure of her skills as the famous doctor seemed to be of his. "Thank you."

"Did you have any symptoms before you fainted?" he asked, lifting the glass of iced tea the waiter had placed before him, his attention focused and sharp. "Chest pain? Shortness of breath? Tingling in the left arm?"

"I didn't have a heart attack," she informed him. "I checked out fine in that department."

"She was born with a congenital heart condition," her mother supplied. "In a nutshell, her heart is too small for her body. It was little to begin with and stopped growing before she reached adolescence."

His gaze lasered into her again. "A child's heart in a woman's body. How old are you?" he demanded, a frown furrowing a deep groove between his eyes.

"Twenty-seven," she replied, then was annoyed with herself. His forceful manner caused her to answer before she had time to consider that her age was none of his business.

"Hmm." He spoke to her mother. "It's a wonder she's lasted this long."

"I beg your pardon," Susan spoke up. "My health is none of your concern. I have a competent doctor of my own."

"Who?"

She was alert to his probing ways now. She paused as if considering, then told him the man's name, a very prominent internist in Houston.

"He's good," the surgeon admitted. "Did he refer you to anyone for a checkup?"

This was a question she didn't want to answer. She tried to think how to do that without lying.

"Susan?" her mother probed, her worry obvious.

"He referred me to you, if you must know." She raised her eyebrows loftily. "I haven't had time to make an appointment."

"Why are you determined to stay in denial about this?" he asked softly. "It isn't your fault."

"I know that. Other than that one little dizzy spell, I've been fine. I just overdid it that week."

"Could you make time to see her?" Kate asked.

"Mother, I'm sure Dr. O'Day doesn't carry around an appointment book with him. His office would handle that."

"Michael," he told her almost sternly. "My name is Michael."

"To your patients?" she challenged.

Her mocking tone didn't seem to bother him at all. He simply nodded, his eyes studying her again. He made her uncomfortable, as if he could see all her doubts, her weaknesses, her furious questioning of God that she should have to give up the only thing in her life.

No. She wouldn't give up dancing. Never! She would, quite literally, rather be dead.

"I'm heading back to Houston Monday morning. I could see you that afternoon, get an idea of how serious a problem you have." He leaned close and looked her in the eye. "Isn't it better to know the truth? Then you could deal with a certainty rather than an unfounded fear."

She glanced at her mother, not wanting to upset her. "I'm not afraid. I've never been afraid of anything."

He leaned back in the chair. She noticed his hands when he lifted his glass. They were incredible, the fingers long and very slender, like a world-renowned pianist's hands, dexterous, capable of performing minute movements very fast and accurately.

She thought of those hands on her—and not in a medical context. Her heart suddenly pumped hard, and for a second, she was frightened. For a second, she thought of accepting his offer to see her.

But only for a second, then reason reasserted itself. She'd lived for twenty-seven years with her heart doing everything she demanded of it. She was fine, just fine.

"If you want a ride back to Houston, be at the airport Monday at nine."

"Oh, how nice," her mother cooed, fawning over the man. "Isn't that convenient?"

"Very," Susan agreed, with absolutely no intention of accepting either the ride or the examination.

His lazy smile said he knew every idea that flitted through her head. She understood him, too. He thought she was a silly, stubborn female refusing to face facts.

It would be a cold day in you-know-where before she'd get within a mile of him, his plane or his office.

"Excuse me," her mother said. "I see a friend."

Susan shifted warily at being left alone with him.

"Don't worry. I'm not the big-bad-wolf type," he murmured, again reading her accurately.

She forced herself to relax. She'd played these games before. It meant nothing. "What type are you?"

"Honest. Sincere. Basically harmless."

To her surprise, she laughed. "No conceit in your family, right?"

His smile disclosed white teeth, even on top, but with one slightly out of line on the bottom. It made him more real, she observed, not quite so movie-star perfect.

She gasped when he laid a hand on her wrist.

"Easy." He proceeded to take her pulse, then looked at her gravely. "Almost a hundred beats per minute."

Jerking away from the incredibly gentle touch that spread fire through her skin, she informed him, "It's none of your business. You aren't my doctor. I'm not going with you Monday—don't expect me to be at the airport."

"So, you like causing your family concern. Because it keeps you the center of attention?"

"Oh," she muttered. "You...you..."

"Baboon?" he supplied, lightly tossing the word out, his ego obviously not dented in the least.

Refusing to dignify the situation with an answer, she stared out at the eighteenth green where two couples completed their game.

A mist blurred her vision for a second. She swallowed hard as agony, which she could usually hold at bay, rushed over her.

"There are other things in life besides dancing,"

he said softly, his fingers gliding along her forearm as if to soothe the troubling emotion.

She recoiled from any possible pity he might feel toward her. "Not for me," she stated, staring him straight in the eye.

He shrugged and rose. "It's your life. But my offer still stands." He walked off.

Two

Sunday morning, Michael arrived at the country club with fifteen minutes to spare before tee time. He grabbed his golf bag and joined Flynt Carson and Tyler Murdoch in front of the pro shop.

"Spence can't make it," Flynt informed the other two. "He's tied up on a case."

"The Carl Bridges case, I assume," Tyler muttered.

Michael didn't know Tyler all that well, but he liked and respected what he'd seen of him. The man was an engineer of some kind for the military. There was a darkness about him, a fierceness that could be intimidating in his hawklike glance. He played one hell of a game of golf and had the lowest handicap of any of them.

"I would guess so. Matt is going to join us," Flynt continued. "If he can tear himself away."

Michael grinned along with the other two men. He wondered what it was about newlywed bliss that mellowed out men. Both Flynt and Matt showed signs of going soft in the head since their marriages.

It wasn't something he and Tyler were apt to experience. They were dedicated career men.

"I heard Michael here isn't a possible father to Lena," Tyler continued. "I finally grabbed a minute and went over to the clinic for the test. We'll know in a few days if I'm a match." He snorted in obvious disbelief.

Flynt checked his watch, then peered down the road with a frown. Matt was late. Michael glanced at the clock behind the desk where the golf pro looked over some papers. They had two minutes until they were supposed to tee off.

Tyler yawned and stretched. "I'll give you ten to one that the unknown daddy is ol' Luke."

"You think?" Flynt questioned affably.

"Damn right," Tyler affirmed. "He's probably off with some gal at a tropical island getaway right this moment. The P.I. we hired will have a time following Luke's path among women the world over."

"I admit Luke disappears pretty regularly. The only thing predictable about his comings and goings is that they are totally unpredictable," Flynt explained to Michael.

Michael knew of Luke's reputation as an international playboy. The multimillionaire could afford the lifestyle.

"Anybody going to take my bet?" Tyler demanded. "A hundred dollars on Luke is my offer."

"Not me," Flynt said.

"Nor me," Michael echoed. "It's time to go. Do we give up our slot and wait, or head out?"

"We'll start," Flynt decided. "Matt can catch up."

The three claimed their golf cart and headed for the first tee. Running footsteps warned them of Matt's arrival a few seconds later. "Sorry," he puffed, tossing his bag into the back of the cart. "Rose was sick this morning."

Michael nodded. "It's common with preg—" He broke off, worried that Matt might not want to discuss his bride's condition.

"Pregnant women," Matt finished. "I know, but I've never been around one before. It's alarming."

While Flynt and Matt discussed pregnancy and its symptoms with great earnestness, Tyler rolled his eyes and winked at Michael, who chuckled as he walked up to the tee and hit his first ball of the day.

All in all, a satisfying game, he thought later, heading for the Yellow Rose Café and lunch after coming in second, right behind Tyler. Sunshine. Golf. Friends. The good life.

Matt called home on his cell phone once they were seated. "Rose is fine," he reported when he hung up. "She's having lunch with her mom and sister."

"I met Susan Wainwright yesterday," Michael told them. "She called me a baboon after I nearly ran her down in the street. I hope Rose is easier to deal with than her sister."

He immediately regretted the lapse in good manners, and even a possible doctor-patient relationship, assuming the stubborn ballerina showed up tomorrow for the checkup.

Matt didn't seem to notice the criticism of his new sister-in-law. "The sisters are diametrically opposite. Rose is gentle and kind...well, not that Susan isn't," he hastily amended. "She's had a lot on her mind of late."

"The heart condition?" Flynt asked.

"Yes. She's been taken off the ballet roster until she has a thorough checkup and her doctor's written okay to return. She's pretty mad about that. Rose is worried." Matt looked at Michael. "You know, you might talk to her and see if you can make her listen to reason."

Michael gave his friend a skeptical smile. "I already offered my services. After our little run-in, I think it would take a major miracle before she would see me."

Daisy, the same waitress from the previous day, came by to take their orders. The place was rapidly filling up, and she looked a bit harried. Michael wondered if she had a crush on Flynt. She was staring at him in an intense way that sent up a caution flag.

Should he warn his golfing buddy to watch out for her?

"Listen, could you come to dinner tonight at the ranch?" Matt suddenly asked, disrupting Michael's thoughts. "Maybe you could reassure Rose, answer some questions for her about Susan's condition. Susan will be there," he added.

"I really don't know much about it."

Flynt added his invitation. "I think you should join us. Josie was asking about you this morning. She read an article in some magazine and was impressed with your credentials. I might be jealous," he warned.

"Right," Michael said wryly. He had nothing better to do that evening. The idea of confronting the haughty Wainwright daughter appealed to him. "What time's dinner?"

"Come at six for cocktails," Matt immediately said. "I'll tell Rose to expect you."

Michael made a mental note of the time and nodded.

"Hey," Tyler said sotto voce. "There's Carmine Mercado. The goon who shot Carl Bridges supposedly works for him. I understand he denies all knowledge of the man."

Michael did a quick once-over of the mob boss as the man left the temporary structure housing the Men's Grill, a cigar clamped between his teeth.

The doctor in him noted the pasty grayness about the mouth and bags under the Mafia don's eyes. He knew Mercado was in his sixties. At one time, the older man would have been described as portly. Nowadays he would be termed overweight and out of shape. He certainly ought to lay off the smoking, Michael observed, listening to the hacking cough as the man and his crony headed for the door.

Abruptly Mercado stopped.

Michael had the uncomfortable feeling Mercado was staring at him. He glanced at Flynt. His friend raised his eyebrows as if to say he hadn't a clue what the older man was looking at.

Mercado entered the café and threaded his way between the tables, garnering irritated glances as he puffed on the stogie. Daisy, the waitress, stopped him.

"No cigars allowed in here, sir," she said politely but with an edge to her voice.

There was a brief pause in the general conversation, then it resumed as if the diners remembered some fascinating tidbit they had to share at that moment.

"Wow," Tyler murmured. "The kid's got brass."

The mob boss narrowed his eyes at the blond waitress, then he dropped the cigar into a glass of water on the table nearest him. Fortunately the diners had left only moments before, so no one was offended by the action.

"Thank you, sir," Daisy said in her heavy drawl and went on her way.

"Arrogant son of a bitch," Flynt said, a steely gleam in his eyes as he watched the little scene.

The rest of the diners let out a collective sigh of

relief. Michael felt the tension drop about ten levels in the café.

To his surprise, the older man came to their table. He nodded to Flynt, Matt and Tyler, then looked at him. "You're the heart doctor, right?"

Although Michael was pretty sure the man had been born in the U.S., there was a definite trace of an Italian accent in his guttural tone.

"Michael O'Day, yes."

Mercado stuck out his hand. Michael had no choice but to shake it. He did so, then gave the don a level stare, refusing to be intimidated by the perusal he was getting.

"My doc told me I needed a new heart."

Michael digested this news, which tied in with the pastiness of the man's skin and the quick, shallow breaths he took. "You need to give up smoking," he stated.

The bushy eyebrows, still black although the man's hair was mostly gray, rose as if questioning Michael's sanity to speak to him this way. "I read about you," Mercado continued. "I want you to do the operation."

"I work out of Houston."

"Yeah, yeah, I know." Mercado waved this little inconvenience aside. "I'll come there."

"I take cases only upon referral from other medical professionals," Michael coolly informed the man.

"My doc will refer me."

This was said in such a way that Michael knew there would be no question about it. He suppressed a smile. There was something of a farce in the scene, as if they were all playing parts in a bad movie.

"Good." He pulled out a business card. "Here's my office number. Have your doctor call."

The bushy eyebrows wagged up, then down. He handed the card to the man behind him. "Here, Frank, hold on to this for me. I'll be in touch," he said to Michael, and walked off.

Silence followed his path to the door.

"Damn," Tyler muttered as everyone relaxed again, "I'd hate to have him for a patient. One mistake and you're out of this world. Literally. What will you do if he shows up?"

Michael shrugged. "A patient is a sick person. I don't judge a sick person's personal life." He grinned. "But I sure hope his doctor suggests someone else."

While his friends chuckled, he made a connection between the don and the recent murder of Carl Bridges.

"Wasn't Carl the one who defended you guys when you were accused of negligent homicide in the death of Mercado's niece?" he asked Flynt and Tyler.

Flynt nodded. "Spence and Luke were also involved. We were having a big reunion celebration out at Luke's place, all of us having survived the Gulf War and made it home in one piece. Naturally the beer was flowing pretty freely. For some stupid reason, the four of us and Haley went for a boat ride. The boat overturned, and Haley drowned. Her family used its influence to have us tried for manslaughter. Carl saved our bacon. It was a bad time for everyone.''

Michael dealt with pain on a daily basis, both physical and mental, in his patients and in the relatives who worried about them. He recognized it in his friend and was sorry to have reminded him of the past.

"I was half in love with Haley," Flynt continued softly, sadly. "I guess we all were. She was beautiful, with thick dark hair and flirty eyes and a smile to melt your heart. She was also smart. And funny. She could imitate almost anyone after hearing them once.''

"Could Carl's death have been some kind of revenge thing from the Mercado family?" Michael asked.

Tyler spoke up. "Not for something that happened years ago. They'd have offed him, and probably us, as soon as the trial was over and we walked out of the courthouse. Haley's brother, Ricky, was a friend. He might have intervened with his uncle for us. Who knows?''

* * *

Daisy Parker, aka Haley Mercado, slipped into the lady's lounge, thankful that it was empty at the moment, and slid into a chair.

She crossed her arms over her chest, holding in the need to cry and rant against fate. It had been terrifying to face Carmine Mercado and his henchman, Frank Del Brio, in the café, not that either man suspected who she really was.

When the Mafia boss had approached Flynt Carson's table, she'd wanted desperately to listen in.

Perhaps it had been foolish to return to Mission Creek, which held so many bad memories for her. But along with the pain, there had been one wonderful one, a night so special she would never forget it.

A sob caught in her throat. At present, her life was unbearably lonely, and she longed for an end to this charade. Please, she prayed, let the FBI complete their investigation of the Texas Mafia soon. She wanted the case finished. She wanted an end to spying and trying to overhear conversations as she worked in the café and grill at the posh country club.

More than that, she wanted things that were probably never going to happen—a quiet life, the husband of her dreams, their children happily playing in the sun.

At the thought of home and family, she nearly gave in to her anger and grief. She was positive her own mother had died at the hands of a Mafia en-

forcer. She would help the FBI by finding out anything she could.

Straightening, she vowed to keep her word. Holding in the useless tears, she returned to work.

Later that afternoon, swimming laps in the community pool at Mission Ridge, Michael mused on the
ill mob boss. Carmine Mercado had been dressed in
an expensive suit. His manner had been arrogant, but
with a certain Old World directness not without
charm. It would certainly be interesting to have him
as a patient.

Still smiling at a mental picture of him operating,
with a bunch of thugs milling around the sterile
room, all with tommy guns hidden under their green
surgical scrubs, he went home, showered and shaved,
then dressed in casual slacks and a blue shirt.

Rolling the sleeves up on his arms as he headed
for the garage, his thoughts turned to the ordeal at
hand. Susan Wainwright, at her age and level of
health, would be an ideal candidate for a new heart.

He grinned with wicked humor. She'd be furious
when she saw him at dinner tonight. The idea still
amused him when he arrived at the Carson ranch, all
15,500 acres of it.

Susan heard the purr of an engine and knew Michael had arrived. She wished she hadn't come, but
Rose had asked her to help with the meal, since her

morning sickness was acting up and apt to occur at any time of the day or night.

A funny ping went through Susan at the thought of a child. It wasn't that she was jealous—Rose was the most wonderful sister one could imagine—it was just...

Okay, maybe she was envious, but only a little.

A heaviness swept over her spirits at the lie. This past year, as it became harder and harder to stick to her practice schedule, several truths had crept up on her.

First, dancing was hard work. Few lead ballerinas made it much past thirty, because the job was so hard on the knees and feet. She'd had no injuries in that department, but one never knew when it could happen. Besides, lately she was so tired all the time.

Second, she'd become aware of loneliness in her life. It didn't seem as if she would ever find the one person meant for her, someone who would understand her drive as a dancer and let her live her life.

And third, she'd probably never have children.

Watching Rose and Matt, seeing the glow in their eyes for each other had awakened something inside her.

Envy, yes. But more than that. A longing for something she couldn't exactly define.

A mate?

She grimaced. Most men she met didn't take her career seriously at all. They didn't seem to understand that she'd spent years getting where she was, that she'd started dance lessons when she was four years old. Twenty-three years of unrelenting effort. One couldn't let up for a second and expect to remain at the top of the pyramid.

She'd expended just as much sweat equity in her career as most men had in theirs, and a heck of a lot more than some of them had.

"Hey, Michael." She heard Matt call a greeting to the famous doctor. Her heart pounded furiously.

Arrogant ape, implying she was self-centered and bratty to cause her family concern over her condition.

It was her life, her body, her heart!

Only she could decide what to do about it. So far, she'd done fine, showing their family doctor and the cardiologist from her youth that she could make it with her "child-size" heart.

"The salad's ready," she announced.

Rose glanced up with a smile from the chocolate icing she was spreading over brownies. "Good. The potatoes are done. I turned the oven off. Josie, would you mind taking the steaks out to Matt? Oh, and see if Michael would like a glass of wine or iced tea rather than beer."

"I don't mind at all." Josie smoothed the tablecloth and placed the crystal bowl of floating roses in the center.

Flynt's wife, Josie, was also expecting. There

must be a fecundity in the Texas air these days, Susan thought. Josie was a natural mother. Susan had watched her earlier with Baby Lena, who was asleep in the guest room at present.

"I'll set the table," Susan volunteered, shaking off thoughts of babies and such things. She felt a tad self-righteous about helping her sister. That should show the baboon she was as nice as anyone.

Except she wasn't as nice as her big sister. Nor as beautiful. Rose, with her black hair, violet eyes and fair, delicate skin, was truly lovely. She had depth to her, a quietness within, as if she'd always known who she was and where she was going.

Susan sighed. She'd been something of a rebel, stubbornly packing off to Houston and trying out for a position with the ballet company in spite of her family's conviction that she would never make it, that her health wouldn't let her even if she had the talent.

She brightened. She *had* made it. But now her life's passion was threatened. The dance company director had made it clear she couldn't return without a clean bill of health.

Not only that, she wasn't even allowed to drive. Her license was temporarily suspended due to her collapse, until a doctor determined that she was well enough to manage a car. It was simply too much.

"Hello, Susan," Michael said in a deep voice that caused the tension level in the room to soar.

Although she'd been aware of him entering the house, unexpected tremors vibrated through her, like a string plucked carelessly and too hard by someone who was not a musician. She inhaled sharply, aware of the heightened pulse beating in her temple, and filled her senses with the scent of talc, men's cologne and the freshness of the evening that clung to his powerful frame.

After placing the last plate on the table, she tossed a casual smile his way. "Nice to see you again."

She'd be polite if it killed her. Rose didn't need to be upset by strain between her and this overconfident surgeon. Needing to go between him and the table to return to the kitchen, she hesitated as she eyed the space.

He was about six inches taller than her five feet, eight inches. A perfect height for ballroom dancing, the thought came to her. She loved all forms of the art.

Meeting the intense blue of his eyes, she murmured, "Excuse me," and waited for him to move out of her way.

He didn't.

To her chagrin, he took her hand in his, then laid the fingertips of his other hand against her wrist.

"Don't," she warned.

He counted, then released her hand. "One hundred and five." He informed her of her heart rate as if he'd taken on responsibility for her health.

"I'm not your patient," she whispered in a near snarl.

"Chalk it up to my job. It's worrisome when someone ignores the obvious. How long do you think your heart can keep up that pace?"

She swept past him. Seeing Rose's concerned gaze, she forced a smile and kept her hands by her sides, although the familiar pain stabbed at her chest. She breathed very deeply, willing her body to slow down and relax.

Her pulse was fast only because Michael O'Day, famous heart surgeon, made her so blasted angry. He probably tortured his patients into letting him operate.

At that ridiculous idea, she had to grin. She was letting all this turmoil affect her too much.

"Well," she said when they sat down for the meal, "here we are. Two Wainwrights—" she indicated herself and Rose "—two Carsons—" she nodded toward Flynt and Matt "—and two referees to keep the peace." She gestured toward Josie and Michael.

Susan was pleased when the other five laughed at her little jab about the infamous Carson-Wainwright feud. Their father had been furious when he learned Rose, the sweet, quiet one in the family, was pregnant. He'd nearly had a hemorrhage when he learned the father belonged to the Carson clan.

"Rose is a Carson now," Matt said with obvious satisfaction.

Susan shook her head. "No way. Maybe half and half, but certainly no more."

"These modern women," Michael complained. "Life was simpler when we could just kidnap them and drag them off to join the male's clan."

"In some tribes, the male joined the female's family," Susan said, quick to point out this fact.

A cry from the bedroom had Josie leaping to her feet and fleeing the room, Flynt right behind her.

"Lena," Rose explained.

The couple returned to the dining room carrying a bundle of pink. The baby girl blinked sleepily at the adults, then puckered up again.

"The bottle," Flynt said, and rushed to the refrigerator. He brought a baby bottle to Josie. "Would you like me to feed her so you can eat?"

Josie shook her head. "Please, all of you, don't let your food get cold. This will only take a few minutes."

The surrogate mother fed the hungry little girl while the other adults watched in open fascination.

"How old is she now?" Susan asked.

"About six months, we think," Josie told her. "The doctor said she wasn't more than eight to ten weeks old when she was found. How could her mother bear to leave her?"

Susan pressed a hand to her chest as fresh pain

surged there. How, indeed, could anyone leave a child?

"I operated on a six-month-old in June," Michael said, a pensive look on his face. "He had a hole between the chambers of his heart."

Flynt gave his friend a worried glance. "How did he do?"

Susan's heart did a little dance against her breast-bone when Michael smiled.

"Fine. He was a fighter from the start. Now his mother says she can't keep him out of trouble. He crawls all over the house and gets into everything."

Susan was surprised at how relieved she felt at the happy ending to Michael's story concerning the child. Her eyes were drawn to Baby Lena. Her own mother had almost given up on grandchildren. Justin, her brother, had once been married, but that had ended in divorce and no children. Now they had Rose's baby to look forward to.

At ten, when Rose served coffee and dessert, Susan realized she was really tired. She'd have to wait until everyone left, though, so Matt could drive her home.

As if on cue, Matt spoke up. "Uh, Michael, would you mind dropping Susan off at her place on your way home?"

"Not at all." Michael leveled a sardonic glance on her. "I probably should go since I have to return to Houston in the morning. If you're ready, Susan?"

She realized there was absolutely nothing she could say but yes. She hugged her sister, told Josie what a lovely job she was doing with Lena, bid the Carson brothers good-night and allowed Michael to escort her from the house.

In the car, with moonlight softly illuminating the landscape and the cool night air flowing through her hair, Susan fumed silently, determined not to quarrel or even speak for the duration of the ride. Thank goodness it wouldn't be long, for the Wainwright ranch adjoined the Carson spread along one side.

"Is it too windy?" he asked. "Shall I put the top up?"

"I'm fine."

"It was a good thing Flynt took the baby, wasn't it?"

"I suppose."

"The foundling brought Josie into his life. She's been good for him, I think, just as Rose had been good for Matt."

"Mmm," she said.

Michael enjoyed needling her into conversation, such as it was. He had to fight a grin as her answers grew shorter and shorter. "Why don't you say what you're thinking before you explode?" he suggested.

"And what is that?" she asked haughtily.

"That you'd rather ride on a bony mule than in a car with me."

"Personally, I can't see much difference."

That did it. He burst into laughter while she flashed him a killing glance from those cool green eyes. "I've always been attracted to a woman of quick wit and a fiery temperament," he murmured.

He was certainly attracted to this woman, he admitted. Flames singed his insides as they rode through the balmy September night. He had the feeling she wasn't indifferent, either, although she pretended he didn't exist at the moment, focusing her attention on the moonlight-flooded fields.

"Beautiful night, isn't it? If we were a couple of kids on a date, I'd be looking for a parking spot about now. Maybe under those pine trees over there."

"You'd get pine sap on your car," she informed him.

"For you I'd chance it," he goaded, his voice lowering to a sexy, husky level that he hadn't intended.

Arriving at the entrance to the Wainwright ranch, he turned in, then stopped in front of a sprawling white ranch house reminiscent of South Fork on the old TV series, *Dallas*. He wondered which bedroom was hers.

She had the door open almost before he stopped. When she headed for the house entrance, he was hot on her heels. With a deliberately casual air, he grasped her arm as if to make sure she didn't stumble and fall into the lush landscaping bordering the front walk.

"Thanks for the ride," she said politely. It was an obvious dismissal.

Something stubborn reared up inside him. "No trouble," he murmured, then did something he'd never done before: he kissed an unwilling woman.

Bending slightly forward, he lowered his head and brushed his mouth over hers, softly, teasing her and perhaps himself because of the sparks that flashed between them now and that had from that first encounter in the street.

If he had any sense, he'd run as fast as he could in the opposite direction from this beautiful young woman with her lithe dancer's body and her fierce anger at the unfair hand she'd been dealt.

Instead of slapping his face as he half expected, Susan stood perfectly still during the first brief kiss, then another...and another.

It was hard to stop, to give up the softness of her mouth, to ignore the tremor in her sensitive lips or the unconscious invitation when they parted in an audible sigh. Caressing her neck, he felt the telltale pounding of a pulse that spoke of the danger she was determined to deny.

"You can't fight fate," he advised gently as he finally surrendered her mouth. "You'll only hurt yourself."

Her chin shot up. "So you say. How much do you get for performing heart surgery?"

"A lot," he admitted, not taking offense at her intended insult.

She went inside and closed the door quietly but firmly in his face.

Michael drove home, no longer aware of the moonlight, but thinking instead of the precarious nature of life itself. There was a sense of urgency in him, as if he needed to do something right away.

Like make love to Susan Wainwright before she disappeared into a wisp of moonlight?

He gave a wry grimace at the absurdity of this notion as he parked and depressed the remote to close the garage door behind him. Two shadows stepped out of the gloom of the dim interior.

"Easy, Doc," one of them said. "We need to have a little talk."

Three

"Do I know you?" Michael asked when he stood face-to-face with the two men in his living room.

Both men wore suits and ties. One, obviously several years older than the other, had a diamond pinky ring. From their appearance, Michael didn't think this was a burglary.

"You know Carmine Mercado," the spokesman of the duo informed him.

"Ah." He indicated the comfortable grouping of chairs. "Have a seat, gentlemen. Would you like a brandy?"

The two men exchanged a glance and nodded. Michael poured each of them a brandy and one for himself, then joined them. "I suppose Mr. Mercado has more questions."

"Nah," the younger man said.

"Maybe," the older one corrected. He leaned forward, his manner suddenly earnest. "He needs a heart."

Michael nodded. "So he said."

"His doc tells him he probably won't get one because of his age."

Michael nodded again. The don had little hope unless a perfect match came in and there was no one younger and healthier who could use it. Fat chance of that happening.

"How does a half mil strike you?" the mobster asked.

"As in, half a million dollars?"

"That's right."

"Sorry, I don't follow you. What's the half mil for?"

"For the operation," the older man said impatiently. "You arrange for the operation, get the hospital to agree and the money will be deposited in your name in any bank in the world, plus the insurance will pay your regular fee."

Michael swirled the brandy, then took a sip, letting it glide across his tongue while he composed an answer.

"Tell Mr. Mercado I'm sorry," he said, and truly meant it. A man's life hanging in the balance wasn't a joking matter, no matter how that life was lived. "It isn't up to me. There's a hospital medical board that decides who gets the next available heart, provided a match comes up. You do understand that there are several blood factors that have to match before we can even take a chance on surgery?"

"Huh."

Michael wasn't sure what the grunted answer meant. He waited for their next move, not at all threatened by their presence now that he knew they were sent by Mercado. The Mafia boss controlled his operations and his minions with an iron fist in a velvet glove, or so he'd heard.

"So, you're refusing to do it?" the older mobster asked, his eyes narrowed.

"I didn't say that. Mercado has my office number. Tell him to call me tomorrow afternoon. I'll be glad to explain how the system works." Michael stood, dismissing the men.

The older thug set the half-full brandy glass on the coffee table. The younger one polished his off in a final gulp before standing when his superior did.

Michael walked the men to the door and politely held it open for them. "Good night, gentlemen."

"By the way, Doc, you forgot to set your security alarm." The thug smiled before stepping outside.

Michael nodded once in response. In truth, he never armed the device. He had very little in the house to steal.

After locking the door, he returned to the living room and picked up his brandy glass. It occurred to him that the goons had no doubt searched every inch of his house.

They probably had a wax impression of his front door key or the code to his garage door opener or whatever means the Mafia used nowadays to enter a person's house unbidden.

He laughed at the absurdity of the situation. Susan

Wainwright and Carmine Mercado. His life was definitely getting interesting.

Susan paced restlessly in front of the hangar. She wouldn't be here at all except for the constant worry she saw in her mother's eyes. So she would let the arrogant Dr. Michael O'Day do a few tests, conclude that her heart was doing just fine and that would be the end of it.

A niggle of fear belied that conclusion.

"Well, hello," a surprised male voice said.

Every nerve in her body twitched at the sound of the indecently sexy tone. "Hi," she said grumpily. "It should be a crime to sound so cheerful this early in the morning."

Michael glanced at his watch as he opened the hangar door. "The sun was up hours ago."

His light-blue gaze swept over her, making her heart speed up. She willed it to a normal beat.

"No luggage?" he asked.

"No. My apartment is in Houston, along with my city clothes. I keep my ranch duds here."

"Good thinking. Come inside. It'll take me a few minutes to run through the checklist."

She observed him as he went through the routine of the preflight check, his attention totally focused on the job.

He wore light-blue slacks and a white polo shirt with blue edging on the collar and sleeves this morning. A bit of silver gleamed among the strands of black hair as sunlight shone briefly on him when he moved around the front of the plane.

"Yo, Doc," another man called and came over to them.

Susan exchanged greetings with the handsome black man dressed in baggy shorts and a leather vest when Michael introduced them.

"Chuck is the best airplane mechanic in these parts," Michael explained. "He manages the airstrip, too."

Chuck accepted the praise as his due. "I checked the engines over on this baby. She's cool, man."

"Thanks." Michael put the checklist in the plane. He glanced her way. "You can board, if you like, then I'll push the plane out."

"I'll help," she volunteered.

His grin was quick, charming and easy. "Okay."

She was relieved he didn't argue or make a fuss about her heart. Her father and brothers would hardly let her lift a finger when she was at the ranch.

The three of them pushed the plane into position. She and Michael climbed aboard. She waved at Chuck, who gave her a thumbs-up sign and an approving smile. She wondered if he thought there was more to her being with Michael than a doctor-patient relationship.

Stealing a glance at her companion as he completed the checklist then taxied to the runway, she wondered the same. Those fleeting kisses, hardly more than the lightest glissade across her lips, had left her sleepless last night.

As the plane rose, she watched the landscape fall away. "There's our ranch," she said.

"Shall we buzz it?"

"Is it legal?"

"As long as we don't get caught."

With a chuckle, he swooped down on the ranch house. Susan waved to the ranch hands as they walked toward the stable. "Oh," she said, seeing someone else.

"What?"

"Nothing."

Michael dipped the right wing so he could see what she was staring at. "Who is he?" he asked, spotting the man fixing a flat by the side of the road.

"Hawk Wainwright."

"You can't just drop it at that," he told her in that gentle way he had when he knew a person was upset.

"My father had an affair with someone. A Native American woman. Hawk was the result. I never knew of him until he moved here and took a job at a nearby ranch."

"Is he why your parents divorced?"

"Yes. My mother found out when I was a baby. My father admits nothing, but Hawk bears his name and...and there is a family resemblance. The three legitimate kids, Justin, Rose and myself, have never known how to handle the situation, so we've mostly ignored him. He's pretty standoffish, too. It must be terrible to be an outsider to your own family—'' She stopped abruptly. Hawk was a family secret that no one talked about.

"Yeah, tough,'' Michael agreed.

She appreciated his sympathetic yet nonjudgmental tone. "We lived in Houston while growing up, but Mother moved back here to be near her family a couple of years ago. Father remodeled a house on the ranch for her. She stays there when she's not in Houston. I think they still love each other, but…''

"It's hard to forgive and forget?''

"Yes.''

"Would you?'' he asked.

A chill attacked her neck at the softly spoken question. She shook her head. "I think women still require fidelity in a marriage. Otherwise, why bother?''

"Yet, in a recent report in a medical journal, twenty-eight percent of the DNA tests for paternity turned out not to be the reputed father's, but some other man's kid. Females don't appear to be much more faithful than males.''

"That number doesn't extend to the whole female population. Those were cases in which paternity was already being questioned. I think it's pretty revealing that in seventy-two percent of them, from marriages that were obviously in trouble, the child *was* the husband's.''

''A point well taken,'' he conceded.

''You said that once before, on Saturday when you nearly ran over me.''

''You have a good memory.''

His eyes met hers. They suddenly seemed darker as thoughts she couldn't read darted through them. She pulled her gaze away from the mesmerizing quality of his.

''I'll never marry,'' she said, then was appalled at herself. Why should he care?

''Why's that?''

''I don't have time for a husband or children.''

''Mmm,'' he said. ''Childbirth would probably be too much of a strain on your present heart, but with a new one, once past the early rejection stages, there's no reason you couldn't have a normal life.''

''My normal life is ballet,'' she reminded him.

''You might have to give up professional dancing,'' he told her. ''But you could probably teach.''

The unvarnished truth was a bitter pill to swallow, she found. ''You can afford to be sanguine about it, but this is my life we're talking about.''

''I'm always truthful with my patients, Susan,'' he said quite gently.

Tears stung her eyes. She forced them back and managed a laugh. ''Maybe we'd prefer a little less honesty.''

He considered, then shook his head. "I would never lie to you. Perhaps you're more courageous than you think. I think you're capable of taking whatever fate dishes out."

She wished she was as sure. However, she discovered she did feel better about this trip and the possible diagnosis the famous Dr. O'Day might give her.

"I haven't agreed to an operation," she quickly reminded him. "I'm only here because of my mother. And my grandmother. She's nearly ninety, but her mind is good. They ganged up on me yesterday." Her laughter sounded more like a nervous whinny. "So I agreed to see you because of them, because I care about them."

"Of course," he said smoothly, and began the descent into Houston.

"How long have you been having chest pains and shortness of breath?" Michael asked on Thursday.

It was after five. His office was closed and only his most stubborn patient was still there. He'd asked Susan to come over after hours to discuss the results of the tests she'd had taken that week.

She tilted her head to one side. "Who says I am?"

For a second he actually considered kissing that mulish expression off her lovely face, but that might lead to other complications and he couldn't afford them.

Monday, he'd had a hard enough time doing his job when he'd had her undress and put on an examining gown. Listening to the erratic beat of her heart had made his own go a little crazy. Barely touching her smooth skin had conjured up visions of climbing onto the table with her and making love instead of checking her health.

He hadn't had those kinds of problems with a patient since his early days in medical school. He smiled grimly to himself. Sometimes his job was tougher than usual.

"You can lie to your parents and yourself, but not to your doctor," he chided, injecting a hint of humor into the moment. It didn't work.

"You don't know everything."

Denial was common in patients with serious conditions. To make progress, she had to get past that. As with the death of a loved one, a person had to go through the stages of grief before acceptance could come. Coming face-to-face with your own mortality wasn't easy.

Susan wasn't at that point yet.

But it would have to come. And soon. He decided on brutal honesty. He laid the reports in a neat pile on his desk, his eyes locked on hers. "If you try to continue your present lifestyle, I'll give you three months. If you take it easy, you might have a year."

She looked stunned. "What? What are you saying?"

"The tests indicate your heart is failing. It drops beats regularly. You didn't get five minutes into the stress test before you became dizzy and weak. You have angina and shortness of breath. How much plainer can I get? In how many more ways does your heart have to warn you it needs help before you listen?"

He had to give her credit. She didn't blink. She didn't cry or curse or do any of the things a patient usually did.

Lifting her chin, she said, "I see. Well, I suppose I'd better get my affairs in order. Isn't that what you tell terminal patients—to get everything sorted out?"

He shrugged. "I find most patients do as they please without hints from me."

Her eyes flashed green fire. Fox fire. Again he suppressed an urge to kiss her into...what?

Acceptance of her fate? Acceptance of his touch?

Turning away abruptly, he pocketed the charts in her folder and laid them in the file basket. "Your life is in your hands. You'll have to decide the future."

"If I have a transplant, won't I have to take medication the rest of my life?" she asked, her manner now almost subdued.

He liked the fire better. "Probably. A lot at first, then it'll gradually taper down as your body learns to live with the new heart."

"Quits fighting the alien invasion, don't you mean?"

Ignoring the sarcastic question, he stood. "Would you like to join me for dinner?" He hadn't realized he meant to ask until that moment.

She shook her head. "I'm going to watch the new ballet the company is putting on tonight."

"A classic, or one of those modern things I never seem to understand?"

"We call it fruit salad," she replied with an endearing little laugh. "A mixture of light, fun pieces from a variety of ballets. Pure fluff, but audiences love it."

He liked her sharing this little insight with him, as if he, too, were an insider to the workings of the art form.

After she departed in that fluid, effortless manner she had, he dictated a report on her condition. The computer printed it out. After reading it over, he placed it in an envelope, put a stamp in the corner and stuck it in his pocket. He'd been asked for the report by Friday. The ballet director should get it tomorrow if he mailed it tonight.

Taking the letter with him, he walked the two blocks to his condo. His pad was on the fourteenth floor, a nifty but rather plain two-bedroom penthouse that was convenient to the office, the hospital and the gym where he worked out while in Houston.

No one had ever spent the night there with him, except his nineteen-year-old niece, Janis.

Ironically the youngster was also avid about ballet and wanted to come to Houston to study dance, but her dad, who was his brother and some twenty years older than himself, was against the idea. Her parents wanted her to stay at the University of Hawaii.

Jim and his wife lived in Hawaii, and they naturally wanted their daughter close. Michael could identify with that, even though he'd never had a close family life himself.

For a moment, nostalgia rolled over him. Recalling his evening at Matt's house with Susan and the other couples, he considered the camaraderie of the Carson brothers. It was one of the things that he'd noticed about the whole family when they had all showed up in mutual support of their father during his bypass surgery.

A nice family, he concluded, made even nicer by the addition of Josie and Rose and the expected babies.

Changing his direction, he decided to go to the gym for an hour and work off the restless energy that plagued him. Oh, one other thing. He dropped the envelope into the mailbox on the corner next to the gym.

There. The grisly deed was done.

He smiled grimly. Now it would be a race between

who would finish him off first: Susan Wainwright or Carmine Mercado. He was personally betting on Susan.

"Tell him Susan Wainwright is here," Susan told the polite but implacable doorman who wouldn't let her go farther than the lobby of the expensive condos.

She glared at the polished pink granite tiles on the floor and the wall housing the elevator. She knew that Michael lived on the top floor.

The penthouse, where he seduced unsuspecting women, she added with vicious sarcasm.

"Uh, he says you're to go right up," the doorman finally told her, hanging up the phone.

The man briskly opened the elevator, saw her inside and punched a button on the panel before stepping back into the lobby and watching as the doors slid closed.

Susan crossed her arms while she rose with smooth speed to the fourteenth floor. When the doors slid open, she stepped out into a large granite foyer with flowers and palm trees, illuminated by a skylight. Chaises and padded chairs were placed at strategic points, making the space seem like a formal living room. Four penthouses opened off the foyer.

Michael stood at one solid oak door. "Welcome to my humble home," he said, a half smile on his lips. He gave a little bow.

"Huh" was her reply to his mock graciousness.

She sailed inside when he stepped back and waved her in.

She stopped abruptly. The lights of the city were laid out at her feet, a banquet of sparkling jewels wrapping around the living room in a breathtaking sweep through floor-to-ceiling windows that lined two sides of the elegant room. She had only to stoop and grab a pocketful of riches.

"Beautiful, isn't it?" he said softly behind her.

She became aware of his body heat along her back. When she stepped forward, then turned, she found his eyes on her.

Pain, sharp and hungry, speared through her.

It seemed unfair to find all this loveliness, to find *him,* at this moment in her life.

"It's very nice," she murmured, getting herself under control and dismissing the ache of passionate need, the longing that confused her.

"Have you eaten?"

She hadn't thought about food since her meeting with the director of the ballet company. "No."

"Good. I put a chicken on the grill earlier. There's plenty—"

"Why did you tell the director I couldn't dance again?"

He paused at a wide archway leading into a modern kitchen made for today's entertaining. A black glass cooktop was set into an island dividing the kitchen from the living room. The host or hostess could prepare a meal and talk to guests at the same time.

"Mmm, she got the letter," he said, nodding as if approving the swiftness of the postal service.

"A medical directive, she called it." Susan was so angry, she could hardly speak. "You went behind my back—"

"Hardly," he interrupted in a harder tone. "I did my job, the one I was paid to do by the insurance company. The ballet director sent me the forms after I spoke to your regular doctor on Tuesday."

"You had no right to fill out any forms," she informed him, her voice shaking, she was so furious.

This time he spoke very gently. "I did."

"I didn't take those tests as a patient of yours. I only did it to appease my family."

His eyebrows rose at this proclamation. She realized in going with him to his office or the hospital or wherever he told her the past week, she had indeed become his patient.

He poured a glass of white wine and set it on the pink-and-black granite counter of the island, pushing it toward her. He refilled his own glass, then prepared another salad to join the one already made. He heated a frozen Duchess potato in the microwave.

Indicating the potato, he said, "Sorry. I take a lot of shortcuts. You may as well sit down. I'm not going to discuss this on an empty stomach. You look as if you need to settle down, as well."

"I'm fine," she said, hardly able to move her jaw.

His unexpected smile almost dissolved her fury at being tricked by him and the ballet director. Tears rose, nearly choking her as she thought of her future.

Which didn't exist.

She had lived for the ballet so long she couldn't imagine what she would do with her time if she never danced again. Pressing a hand to her chest, she willed the momentary weakness away. She was fine. Fine.

Michael came around the island and wrapped her in his arms, as if sensing her uncertainty. "I'll take very good care of you. I'll make the surgery as easy as I can."

For a few seconds she let herself relax in his embrace. It felt so good to put herself in his capable hands and not have to think anymore. Her heart settled into a rhythm with his.

"Susan," he said, his voice deep and quiet and compelling, but so gentle.

So very gentle it almost made her weep. She tilted her head against his arm and stared into eyes that suddenly seemed a darker blue. She wanted to speak, to ask him…something, but she could only think of his name.

"Michael," she whispered, and heard the longing she could no longer deny.

His chest lifted against her breasts as he pulled

in a deep breath. "You could make me forget," he said.

"Forget what?"

"My oath to do no harm," he muttered cryptically.

She couldn't wait any longer. Rising on her toes, she took the kiss, as hungry as a newborn for nourishment.

He gave a deep, throaty growl and pulled her closer into his arms. The kiss deepened, becoming ever more demanding as hunger rampaged between them.

She wished she'd met this man long ago, back when she was young and was positive she could have all of life her own way. The fierce hunger added to the pain that seemed to fill her soul of late.

When he sought entrance to her mouth, she gave it eagerly, then followed his tongue in sensual play. At last she became aware that she couldn't get enough air. She moaned and moved her head slightly.

He released her mouth, permitting her to breathe deeply, while he trailed kisses along her jaw, her ear, her throat, down to the open collar of her dress. Heat infused her all the way to the cold inner spot that had formed when she'd collapsed onstage. With this man, she felt strong and invincible once more.

"So different," she murmured, perplexed by all

the emotion and sensation that assailed her. "Why? Why is it different with you?"

His soft laughter made her breasts ache for him, her nipples harden. She wanted more from him.

"Because it was meant to be. Some things can't be denied." He lifted his head and stared into her eyes. "This is one of them."

"I'm not denying it," she told him, reminded that he'd accused her of being in denial about her heart. "It's real...this passion, the hunger you bring into being." She tried to look away but couldn't. "It isn't a good time."

"The timing may not be perfect, but it would be good," he promised, passion making his eyes flame with unconcealed need. "Between us, it would be very good."

She pressed her forehead to his chest and tried to recall the anger. "You betrayed me. You wrote the letter that destroyed my life."

"No. I did my job. I'll never do less than the best I can as a doctor. Nothing and no one can change that."

He tipped her face up so he could study her. She met his unrelenting perusal, the demand in the depths of his eyes and knew what he wanted from her.

Pain, harsher than any she'd ever experienced, washed over her in a sickening wave. "I won't," she whispered, pulling away from his comforting embrace. "My heart has worked fine for twenty-seven years."

"It's failing now."

She couldn't let herself believe that. "Liar."

"I'm not the one in denial."

Words failed her. She shook her head and pulled away from the warmth and security in his embrace. She wanted to run. She wanted to stay. She wanted him to take away the pain and give her life back.

Retreating, she grabbed her purse and rushed toward the door. "You don't know," she whispered almost on a sob. "You just don't know."

"I do," he contradicted in the very gentle manner he sometimes displayed. "I do know. Don't go."

But she had to. He was too compelling, too attractive, too many things, none of them meant for her.

She fled.

Four

Michael debated following Susan, but decided against it. She needed time to cool down, think things through, then accept the inevitable. He had no doubt that she would. She was too candid to lie to herself for long.

The phone rang.

He muttered an expletive. He didn't want to deal with a life-and-death emergency tonight. However the call wasn't from the hospital or his answering service.

"Hey, Doc," the doorman said. "Uh, that lady that came to see you..."

"Susan. Yes?"

"Well, when the elevator door opened, she was lying on the floor—"

"What?"

"She like fainted or something. Can you come down?"

"Is she still in the elevator?"

"Yeah. I didn't know what to do—"

"Send it back up. I'll take care of her."

"Right," the man said in obvious relief.

Michael waited impatiently in the foyer. As soon as the elevator doors opened, he stepped inside and assessed the situation. Susan was propped in a corner. She opened her eyes when he bent over her.

"I'm all right. Just a little dizzy spell," she mumbled. Her face was white, her lips blue tinged.

"Little fool," he said, and scooped her up.

"I'm fine…" Her head wobbled and fell to his shoulder. She gave a low groan.

He could feel the hard erratic beating of her heart against his chest. Kicking the door closed behind them, he carried her into his condo. In his bedroom, he carefully laid her down on the comforter.

Taking her pulse, he found her heart was working overtime, but she still wasn't getting enough oxygen. Opening the medical bag he always kept with him, he pulled out the cuff and took her blood pressure. High, but not bad, considering the condition of her heart.

With quick movements, he unfastened the belt and buttons on her shirt-type dress and pushed it aside so he could listen to her heart with the stethoscope.

It was dropping beats, then pounding erratically to make up the loss, but the beats were strong enough, not fluttery or weak. No gurgles to indicate valve leakage.

"You're okay," he said. "Just upset. You'll have to give up anger as a defense. Your heart can't take it."

She opened her eyes and he saw the despair before she managed to hide it behind a sarcastic smile. "Dr. O'Day to the rescue. My hero."

"Michael," he said.

She pushed up against the headboard and pulled the edges of her dress together. It was too late. He already knew how enticing she looked in a lacy beige bra and matching panties. She wore no slip. Her legs were long, supple and tanned to a golden hue. He removed her sandals and placed them neatly under his reading chair.

He slipped an arm around her shoulders to lift her up and positioned two pillows behind her back, then lowered her so she could rest on them.

"Are you feeling nauseated?" he asked, forcing himself to step back rather than climb in bed with her.

"No. I'm fine." She frowned. "Maybe a little wobbly."

He could have kissed her for admitting it. A first step for the stubborn ballerina. A big one.

She fidgeted with her buttons, fastening them, but her hands were trembling, making her fingers awkward. He saw no reason to offer to help. She wasn't going anywhere.

"Here, take this." He handed her a pill and fetched a glass of water from the bathroom.

"What is it?"

"Aspirin. To make it easier on your heart."

She hesitated, then took the pill. "Would you call me a taxi?" she requested. "I don't think I feel like walking home at the present."

Her smile was cheeky, but it didn't sway him. "No."

"I want to go home." She glared at him.

"You'll stay here tonight."

"No way."

"Either here or in the hospital. Your choice."

She clenched her fists as if preparing to strike him. Color returned to her face, and her eyes flashed fire. He waited to see which way she would go—fight or flight.

Energy surged through him at the thought of a tussle between them. All his senses went on high alert. He inhaled the light scent of her cologne, the feminine fragrance that was part of her. Blood shot to strategic points in his body, making him very aware of his own heart's clamoring.

"You can't make me—" She stopped as if realizing he possibly could.

"I can," he stated. "After that barrage of tests this week, I'm listed as your caregiver with the hospital and the testing lab. You'd have to fill out a ton of hospital and insurance forms to go against my orders."

"You're despicable."

"Yes." He went to the armoire. "Here are pajamas and a robe. Dinner's in fifteen minutes." He paused and looked her over, a sharp challenge in his eyes. "Don't try to slip out. And don't take a bath. Unless you want me in there to see that you don't faint and drown."

Chuckling at the shock that flitted over her rebellious face, he returned to the meal he'd been working on before her timely—or untimely, according to how one wanted to look at it—arrival. He placed the two Duchess potatoes in the toaster oven to warm, set the table, turned the lights to a soft glow so they could enjoy the lights of the city while dining. Out on the garden patio, he removed the chicken from the grill rotisserie.

After putting the food on the table and pouring them each a fresh glass of wine, he called, "Dinner."

She appeared at once, still dressed and buttoned from neck to hem, the sandals on her feet.

Holding a chair, he beckoned her to be seated. She did so, her back as stiff as a mad cat's.

He played the polite host, inquiring as to her favorite kind of meat, white or dark, then giving her some of each when she indicated it didn't matter. While she picked at the food, he polished off almost all the chicken, along with the potato and a huge serving of mixed salad greens.

"There's frozen yogurt and strawberries for dessert," he told her when she laid the fork on her plate. He didn't comment on how little she'd eaten.

"I don't care for any, thank you."

He carried their plates to the kitchen, put them into the dishwasher, then dished up a big bowl of the yogurt and strawberries and added a large dollop of hot fudge sauce to top it off.

"You should be big as a house," she muttered when he returned to the table.

He grinned. "A growing boy needs sustenance."

Heat erupted low in his abdomen as she raked him over with those green eyes, cool now that she'd calmed down.

When she turned back to the view, he inhaled deeply and willed his libido to quiet down. In letting him perform tests on her, he truly had become her doctor. Only the worst kind of medical practitioner took advantage of the doctor-patient dependency syndrome that could thus develop.

Not that Susan showed any signs of that, he admitted with rueful candor. Just the opposite. She fought him every step of the way. Besides, the attraction had been there from the first, before he knew her as a candidate for surgery.

"Did you mean it when you said you'd give me three months?" she asked after several minutes of silence.

She watched him over the rim of the wineglass as she took a sip after asking the question. A shield, he mused. She was keeping her defenses up.

"It's a definite possibility."

He saw her chest rise and fall in a sigh. Placing the glass on the table, she rubbed the condensation from it, her expression closed but thoughtful. He waited, although he wanted to take her into his arms again and comfort her.

He knew where that would lead.

They were both too vulnerable tonight, and they were too volatile together. He pulled his shredding integrity together and stayed where he was while she considered her options and the ordeal she faced.

"Bite?" he finally asked, and held out a spoonful of dessert.

To his surprise, she took it, delicately wiping off a drop of chocolate from her lower lip with a quick sweep of her tongue. It almost wiped out every bit of his resolve to resist his attraction to her.

They finished off the treat, sharing bites as if they'd done this often. After he straightened up the kitchen, they watched an old movie on TV. He took her pulse and blood pressure again before going to bed.

"Better," he pronounced when she looked at him, concealed anxiety in her eyes. "This will help you sleep."

He gave her a medication that would relax her and induce natural sleep. Her heart needed the rest, as did her mind. Sleep would let her subconscious sort through the tangled emotions and maybe accept her fate.

After she was ensconced in the guest room, along with the pajamas, robe and a toothbrush, he went to his room. Looking at the mussed comforter on his bed, he thought of sleeping there with her. Well, not exactly sleeping.

An hour later, he considered taking a pill himself in order to relax and get some sleep. It had been a long time since a woman had kept him awake. His life had been too busy. Dedicated to his career, he really hadn't thought about marriage and all that it entailed.

And he still wasn't considering it, he reminded himself caustically. Commitment was a big step and he'd already made one—medicine.

Susan woke frightened and disoriented. She stared around the dark room and wondered where she was.

The door opened a crack.

"Are you all right?" Michael asked.

Everything came back to her. She pressed a hand to her pounding chest and sucked in deep breaths until the pain receded. "I was dreaming."

"Yeah, I heard you struggling. Did a monster grab you?"

He came into the room and flicked on the bedside lamp. She saw it was nearly two in the morning.

Ignoring his humor, she shook her head. "It was someplace dark. I couldn't see anything. It was like being blind. And deaf. I was waiting for my cue, but

I couldn't hear the music. I tried to move closer to the stage, to see which ballet we were doing, but it was as if I was glued to the spot. I knew it must be time for me to go on, but something held me back.''

Closing her mouth, she cut off the flow of words before she disclosed too much—the horror of the dream, the terrible, terrible sense of loss, the desperation to take her place onstage, the need to dance until her heart stopped...

"You must have been backstage at the ballet,'' he told her.

A chord thrummed inside her. It bothered her that he understood the dream and what she'd been feeling.

"Turn over,'' he said in a soothing voice.

Before she quite knew how it happened, she was on her stomach, and he was massaging her shoulders through the borrowed pajama top. When he rubbed down either side of her spine with his thumbs, she moaned in ecstasy.

"I'll give you just thirty minutes to stop that,'' she said, the tense muscles relaxing all at once as she tried for a lighter note. The nightmare receded, and she felt safe once more.

He chuckled, a rich sound that reminded her of hot-fudge sauce and other good things. The hunger roiled through her, catching her by surprise. She gasped.

"Did I hurt you?" he asked, easing up on his strokes.

"No."

"Do you need another pill to sleep?"

"No."

"What's wrong?" he asked.

"How do you always know when I'm...when..." She stopped the runaway words before she made a complete fool of herself and willed the need to go away.

"When you're vulnerable?" he asked quietly. "Because you're a fighter, and there's no one to fight."

She turned over and looked at him, and her breath caught. He wore pajama bottoms only. His chest was broad and muscular. A generous covering of black hair swirled over trim, washboard ribs and arrowed down to the waistband.

"Don't look at me like that," he warned, a hint of laughter in the words, but danger, too.

He was an aroused male animal. She knew she shouldn't tempt him too far, but she ignored the warning.

"Make love to me," she whispered.

Regret shadowed his eyes. He shook his head. "I can't. It's not good ethics."

"Ethics be damned." She reached for him.

The kiss was sweet and as hot as a July firecracker. Somewhere in the misty delight, she wondered why she wanted this man, this way, this much. It made no sense to desire the enemy. Except he didn't feel like an enemy.

She ran her hands over his torso—his back, his sides, his chest, down to his abdomen where the muscles tensed like rocks under her fingers.

He caught her hands and held them against the mattress, his weight lightly on her. Their bodies slipped down until she lay on the pillow. She could feel her heart beating, felt that his was just as fast. When he let her mouth go, he pressed his face into her hair.

"You can drive me wild with just a word, a touch," he admitted.

"I've never wanted anyone like this, either. It's totally insane, yet..."

"It seems the only sane thing in a world gone mad," he finished for her. Then he pulled away and sat up. "But it's not going to happen."

She considered, somehow knowing she could push past his defenses if she persisted. It was heady knowledge. Her nipples beaded as fresh hunger rushed through her.

He smiled and with a forefinger gently flicked each tip visible against the cotton of the pajamas. "We're a dangerous combination. Go to sleep, dancing girl, before I forget my good intentions." With that, he left her and closed her door behind him.

Sighing deeply, she let the sexual tension drain out

of her, refusing to see any other reasons for the passion between them. It was all physical attraction, nothing more.

Finally she closed her eyes as sleep claimed her again. She felt oddly secure now. She had only to call out and he would be there. It was a good thing to know.

Susan spotted Michael on the patio as soon as she entered the living room the next morning. He was drinking coffee and reading the paper. She went to the kitchen and poured a cup. Seeing her, he indicated a chair at the glass-topped table. She joined him.

Bagels, cream cheese and jelly were on a buffet table beside the grill. She helped herself.

The air was clear in the city that morning and wonderfully refreshing for this time of September, although it would be hot in the afternoon. October was only nine days away.

She felt her life slipping away with each tick of the clock. And each beat of her heart.

A need to reach out and grab all she could hit her soul in a tidal wave of grief. With an effort, she summoned her composure and the anger that was rapidly becoming her only barrier to the darkness.

"Don't think, because I acceded to your orders last night, that I'm going to do so again," she told him.

He hardly glanced up from the paper. "I wouldn't think of it," he said drolly.

She gave him her meanest glare. He didn't look up.

"Don't think to sway me with sex, either. I admit you're attractive, but I've met lots of handsome men. A few kisses don't mean a thing."

He sighed, folded the paper and laid it aside. "Do say what's on your mind," he invited.

"Doctors don't always know what's best. My grandmother was told she'd be dead of cancer within six months when she was in her fifties. She'll be ninety her next birthday."

"Sometimes remission happens when we least expect it," he conceded. "But, unlike the Grinch who stole Christmas, your heart isn't going to grow three sizes anytime soon."

"It's worked fine for years. Why should it suddenly quit?" she demanded. "Answer me that."

He poured fresh coffee from an insulated carafe, taking his sweet time about replying. She sat perfectly still, as if she, too, had all the time in the world.

Three months. A year.

No wonder she was having nightmares. How dare he calmly tell her something like that! It was cruel.

"Brave heart," he murmured after sipping the hot brew. "You have a hardworking little heart, but it's worn out. Right now, I'd say it's running on courage and little else.''

She fought a wild desire to cry, to fling herself into his arms and sob out her fears and frustrations and fury with the uncertainty that haunted her.

No! she commanded. The tears receded.

''You sound like my family,'' she told him with an edge of cutting humor. ''Susan do this, Susan do that. Listen to your elders. It's for your own good.''

''I'm not that much older than you.''

''But you act like my father—older and wiser and father-knows-best.'' She spat out an expletive that told him what she thought of that.

''Were you always a rebel against authority?'' he asked, sounding perfectly good-natured.

''Always.''

Michael decided there was only one way to handle an obstinate woman. He'd lay the truth on the line for her so she'd have no misunderstanding of what he was saying.

''We've kissed what, two, three, four times?'' he asked.

The question obviously startled her before she remembered to glare at him in distaste, refusing to answer.

''Something like that,'' he continued in a lazy drawl. ''You reacted strongly each time. Like anger, passion is hard on the heart. How are you going to react when your husband tries to make love to you?''

She didn't answer.

He did it for her. "You could faint. Or have heart failure. Have you thought of that?"

"No."

"People laugh when older men have heart attacks while making love, but believe me, it isn't a joke. It's damn scary for him and for his partner. How do you think your husband would react?"

"Since I don't have one, I couldn't say."

"Come on, entertainers have active imaginations. They have to, in order to transport their audiences into their world of make-believe, don't they?"

"You're the great philosopher. You tell me."

What he really wanted to do was sweep her into his arms and take her to his bedroom and show her everything he could make her feel in his arms. It was a temptation, almost more than he could stand.

A light sheen of moisture broke out all over him.

"Having children would be out of the question. You are correct in that."

"I might," she contradicted. "If I rested and ate right." She snapped her fingers. "I know. I could take an aspirin a day. Isn't that the miracle cure nowadays?"

"A fight to the finish," he muttered, admiring her stubborn determination to live life on her terms. He said as gently as he could, "Not for you."

Three months. One year.

Susan felt the words hammer in her brain. Feigning indifference, she finished the bagel and wiped her mouth. "Well, I'm off. Thanks for your hospitality."

"It was a pleasure."

There was such sincerity in his reply, such warmth in his eyes, she believed him. She took her dishes to the kitchen to escape his gaze.

He followed her. "I can give you the miracle you need. Let me put your name on the list for a donor."

Panic raced through her. "I'd rather be dead than never dance again," she said as fiercely as she could to let him know she meant it.

"You have a wonderful talent. Why not share it with others by teaching?"

"I don't want to teach. I want to dance."

"Grow up," he said, suddenly harsh. "You've fulfilled that dream. Go on to another one."

She grasped the edge of the counter and stared down at its smooth surface. "I can't. I'd be someone different."

An invalid.

The hateful word hurled itself from her subconscious into her conscious mind. She would become an invalid, always taking pills, always worrying about a cold, a tiny cut, the least infection that could kill her.

"What kind of life would I have?" she questioned aloud.

Laying his hands on her shoulders, he turned her

to face him. "It could be normal. Humans have an amazing capacity to adapt, you more than most. You have great self-discipline. You'd establish a new life."

Entranced by his belief in her, she was tempted to concede, to simply give in and stop fighting him and her family and those who thought they knew best for her.

"What's in this for you?" she demanded, wanting to hurt him because of the pain he stirred in her.

He gave her a wary, questioning look.

"Money?" she asked. "Prestige? Ah, the wonderful Dr. O'Day. He saved Susan Wainwright, you know. Her family endowed a whole wing of the hospital in his name—"

She got no further in her taunting.

Michael had always been too focused, too busy, to bother with anger, especially with other people. Right now, though, he saw red. It was as if an alien mist had rolled over his mind, taking control of his reactions and his conscience.

He would teach her a lesson.

With a quickness of motion ingrained in him from his work, he lifted and carried her to the sofa. There, he laid her out like a feast prepared just for him. Before she could move, he pinned her by lying partially on her, not enough to crush, but enough to keep her at his mercy.

"Let me go," she demanded.

"Not on your life," he said in an angry snarl.

Her eyes flicked open wide, then she gave him a narrow-eyed frown of warning. He caught her hands and pinned them above her head before she could think of a way to use them he might not like.

He took her mouth when she opened it. He delved inside and felt the exquisite heat that was hers. The mist in his mind thickened to a hot haze of desire.

Against his chest, he felt her nipples contract and knew she felt it, too, in spite of the battle of the wills between them, in spite of both knowing this was insane.

"How will you respond to this?" he asked huskily, and took her breast in his palm.

She tensed beneath him, and he experienced the flex of her strong, lithe, trained body. It was like holding some fluid medium, one of energy and force, but crafted with infinite grace, too.

It was wonderful. It was hell.

Hell—because he knew he couldn't go far enough to appease the raging hunger she released in him. But it would be far enough to teach her a lesson.

With easy movements, he dispensed with the buttons and the belt on her dress, then spread it to either side so that he could look at her. "You take my control to the limit," he said, warning her and himself.

Unable to stand it, he unfastened the delicate bra and lavished attention on the rosy tips of her breasts, sucking at one, then the other, until she moved against him, responding as he'd known she must. Neither of them could deny the need they stirred in each other.

And the anger. He had to hold on to that or he'd let go completely and take them both to paradise.

"Touch me," he ordered.

With a shaky sigh, she yielded to the madness and pushed her hands under his T-shirt. She explored his flesh as if learning to trek through a strange land. When she fingered his nipples, a ripple of longing coursed through him. He sought her lips again.

The kiss went on and on, past lesson-giving, past reason and integrity and all that baggage.

"Ohh," she gasped while he laved hot kisses along her throat. "Come to me."

It was a plea.

He was on fire for her. Some part of him knew he'd slipped beyond—way beyond—the control of his conscience. They were male and female, acting on instincts as old as time and as unrelenting.

Laying his hand on her breast, he felt the beat of her heart. Against his lips, he could feel the wild, harsh pounding of her pulse. He heard the gasps as she breathed. Her hands roamed over him in sensual forays, needy in the desperate yearning that consumed them.

He knew they had to stop.

"Easy," he whispered.

"Now," she demanded, her hands urgent on him.

"No." He kissed her a thousand times, gentle soothing kisses to cool the volcano of need.

"Why? We're both willing."

He heard the perplexed hurt behind the words. "Because it's time to leave. My plane is ready. I'll take you home."

"To Mission Creek?"

"Yes."

He knew the moment sanity returned. Regretfully he eased away and stood, freeing her from their mutual madness.

There would come a time, he was certain, when they wouldn't, couldn't, stop. Then where would they be?

No answer came to him then or on the silent flight to Mission Creek.

Five

"Mother, I'm fine. Really," Susan insisted. She swung her feet off the sofa and sat up. She felt grungy and out of sorts and in need of a shower. Her hair was a mess. She combed a dried grass blade out of it with her fingers.

Both her parents watched her with grave faces. Vaguely she recalled a similar scene from her childhood, her lying in bed, her mom and dad leaning over her, fear in their eyes while they made her lie still. She'd fainted then, too.

The memory came back more clearly. Her family—no, not her father, she recalled, but the rest of them—had been to Lake Maria on a picnic while visiting their grandmother. She'd tried to follow her brother in diving down and retrieving a stone from the very bottom of the lake. The next thing she knew, she was in the hospital emergency room, waking to find both her parents bent over her, worry on their faces. Just as they were now.

"You stay put," Kate ordered. "I'm going to call Dr. O'Day—"

"No!" Susan tried to smile and make light of her

panicky reaction. "There's no need to bother him on a Saturday. This is his time to rest."

She didn't add she'd had all of the obnoxious doctor she could take at the present, thank you very much.

Archy Wainwright, her father, spoke sternly. "I've ordered the ranch hands not to let you ride unless they have my direct approval. You could have broken your neck, falling off a horse the way you did. Scared your mother half to death," he added with a protective glance at his former wife.

Susan sighed and gave it up. "You're right," she admitted, hoping meekness would throw them off track when firmness hadn't. "I'll be more careful from now on. Absolutely no more riding alone. I promise."

She refrained from holding her hand up in a Scout's honor pledge. That would be overdoing it.

"You don't fool me a bit," her mother informed her. "I'm going to call Michael O'Day and ask him to come out for lunch. I want to talk to him."

"No need for you to bother with a meal," Archy said to Kate. "Esperanza is already cooking. I'll tell her to add a plate for you and the doctor."

"Yes, that would be good," Kate said absently, her thoughts obviously on their daughter.

Looking more than a little worried, Archy left the room, but was back in a moment. He directed a steely eye on his daughter. "We'll ask the heart doctor the results of your tests and find out how *fine* you really are.''

Susan flounced off the sofa. ''Since we're going to have a guest, I suppose I'd better shower.'' She rushed to her room before her mother could object.

Once under the steamy water, she thought of Michael and his threat to join her if she tried to bathe alone. The blood pumped furiously through her, making her vitally aware of how much that appealed to her.

Oh, she mentally groaned. She was obsessed with the man. What was wrong with her mind, her dancer's discipline?

Images of him and her at his condo leaped and spun through her brain like the finely executed chaînés she had once done so effortlessly. The visions left her breathless and excited and alarmed.

She had no time for romantic daydreams, not when her career hung in the balance.

And her life, according to him.

Finding it difficult to think of her own mortality, she nevertheless found it worrisome that the dizzy spells were coming more frequently. Perhaps…perhaps she should retire from the active ballet.

At the dismal thought, pain grabbed her and wouldn't let go. What would she do with herself? The days were already endless now that she didn't have practices and performances to gear up for.

Clean and dry, her hair curling under at her shoulders, she stood in front of the full-length mirrors on her closet doors, dressed only in underwear. Her hand on a chair back, she bent her knees in a plié, a grand plié, then executed a small jump, a jeté.

Her heart also leaped.

Grimly, her eyes on the bedside clock, she took her pulse. Slightly over a hundred with just one jeté, and that not even a big one.

Slumping into a chair, she sat there for a long time, waiting for her pulse to slow to its usual eighty to ninety beats per minute, her mind curiously blank as she watched the activity on the sprawling acres visible from the window.

Alfalfa was being cut in one field. In another, it was being rolled into huge round bales of hay. Ranch hands were loading some cattle heading for the market.

Hector Martinez, the gardener, was spraying a bed of roses. His little girl, Maria, held a pair of pruning shears for him. Esperanza, Hector's wife, came outside and talked to them. Maria, under her father's direction, cut a dozen roses and gave them to her mother. Esperanza carried them into the house. They would appear on the table at lunch.

Life as usual on the Wainwright ranch.

But not for her. She wasn't to ride alone, she couldn't drive a car... "Speak of the devil," she muttered.

A light-blue sports car parked in front of the house. Michael climbed out. Her mother had wasted no time in calling the arrogant surgeon, it appeared.

Glancing at the clock, she saw it was time to go down. Quickly slipping into beige slacks, a striped blouse and espadrilles, she headed for the patio.

It occurred to her that her mother was often at the main house of late. Since the ignominious collapse onstage, in fact. Divorced for many years, her parents seemed to have formed an alliance against her.

On further reflection, she realized that Kate, although keeping a condo in Houston, had mostly lived at the ranch for the past couple of years—since returning to Mission Creek to oversee her own mother's move into the senior care facility in town.

Her father had insisted on remodeling a cottage on the place and having Kate stay there "to be near your mother and closer to the children," he'd said when Kate had at first refused.

Since Justin was sheriff and had his own place and Rose was now married to a Carson and lived at Matt's home, that left only Susan as the child at home. Permanently at home?

No, she refused to feel sorry for herself. She wasn't a coward, no matter what Michael thought of her. Life was what it was. She'd figure out a way to live with no problem. Or die trying. On this sardonic note, she went outside.

"Hello," she called, brightly cheerful as she

breezed over to the table to join the others. "Michael, how nice that you could join us." There, that put him firmly in the friends-of-the-family category and not that of her doctor.

After taking her place, she glanced at her father. His face had the closed look he got when he was upset. Her mother's was in its determined mode.

"You and your mother favor each other," Michael murmured to her while her parents were distracted by Esperanza's appearance with a lovely vase of pink roses.

"Yes, we have the same stubborn look, I've been told," she said coolly, with just the right tinge of humor.

"True."

She suppressed the jab of irritation with his easy agreement. She'd be calm if it killed her!

Her father deferred to his former wife when the housekeeper asked where the flowers were to go. After suggesting a side table, Kate turned back to the group. "Dr. O'Day, can you give us a report on Susan?"

"Please, call me Michael," he requested.

He took in the scene with his quick intelligence, Susan noted. Had she not been the topic of discussion, she would have enjoyed him being put on the spot by her mother.

Michael began. "You are both aware that Susan has a small heart."

Archy nodded. "And she had another dizzy spell this morning and fell off a horse."

She hadn't fallen from a horse since she'd been eight and tried to ride a mean stallion on a dare from her brother. This morning, one of the hands had been the first to reach her. He'd quickly examined her for injury, then put her in his pickup and taken her back to the house against her protests. Naturally her father had called her mother, one thing led to another, and now here they were.

"Do I have your permission to give them the results of your tests?" Michael asked.

Reluctantly she nodded.

"Her heart is failing—"

Her mother gasped and pressed trembling fingers to trembling lips. "Easy, Katie," her father said gently.

"When the heart has to continuously work so hard to pump blood, whether from high blood pressure or another reason, it starts breaking down. This is known as congestive heart failure. There's no question Susan will have to have a new one," Michael continued. "She hasn't yet consented to be placed on the list for a donor heart."

"To give up that which works, no matter how imperfectly, for that which might not, seems foolish to me," Susan told him. "What kind of choice is that?"

"A hard one, but necessary."

"Listen to the doctor," Archy ordered, sharing a glance with the younger man.

There was an obvious rapport between the two men. Her father was much older than the doctor, yet the men seemed to be cast from the same steely mold and to communicate on the same level of some masculine code that eluded her.

"How can we convince her this is the right thing to do?" her mother asked.

"I'm on vacation for the next few days. I'll talk to her." Michael shot a grin at Susan. "Will you listen?" he asked, tossing the question at her like a fastball to first base, hoping to surprise the runner there.

With the others watching, what could she say?

"Of course," she managed to get out without throwing a glass of water in the handsome face observing her with wry amusement in his eyes.

He knew he had her at his mercy. She wouldn't be too awfully rude in front of her family. But when she got him alone... The thought brought up a whole list of other things they could do. Furious with her willful mind, she stared at the fields until her heart calmed again.

Esperanza broke the tension by serving a salad topped by bay shrimp. She placed a tray of small crystal pitchers filled with various salad dressings in the middle of the table, along with a basket of fresh bark bread covered with poppy and sesame seeds.

Her oldest daughter, Carmel, pushed a drink trolley onto the patio. The housekeeper served regular or raspberry-flavored iced tea. There was also a carafe of coffee, which could be served hot or cold.

"After lunch, Susan, perhaps you would take Michael on a tour of the grounds," her mother suggested. "The mint along the creek smells wonderful."

Susan tried to think of something compelling she had to do. Nothing came to mind. She could claim stiffness due to the fall. No, that would make her parents worry—

Michael burst out laughing.

Startled, she glanced up and saw everyone watching her. Her parents looked a bit disapproving. Michael, the big ape, was still chuckling. Esperanza and Carmel were smiling.

Heat rushed to her face as she realized they all knew exactly what she was thinking. "I'd be delighted to show Dr. O'Day the mint beds at the creek," she said demurely.

"Michael," he corrected softly.

"The pride of the ranch," Susan said, indicating a herd grazing in the nearest pasture. "Our best brood cows."

"How many head of cattle can you run on a fifteen-thousand-acre ranch?"

"Truthfully, I'm not sure. You'd have to ask my

father. This is natural rangeland. My grandmother says there used to be grass as far as the eye could see, but overgrazing destroyed most of it. Mesquite, creosote bushes and cactus replaced the native grasses.''

"Then settlers brought in citrus and cotton," Michael added. "From the air, you can see miles of groves and fields of white when the cotton is ripe. Did you notice when we flew in?"

"Yes." Since this sounded like a shared bond and she was determined to keep her distance, she walked faster. "This way."

He strolled alongside her as she turned onto the path that skirted the arroyo once filled by Mission Creek, a small stream that flowed down to the Rio Grande. That was before the Carson ancestors had talked the city fathers into damming the creek, thus forming the lake that had cut off the water supply to the Wainwright ranch.

"The creek was the source of the feud between your family and the Carsons, right?" Michael asked, holding a thorny mesquite limb out of their way.

"Part of it. A betrayed love and a suicide started it. Then my great-grandfather shot the Carson great-grandfather. It was tit for tat after that, conniving to outsmart each other and cattle rustling between them."

"So where does the water come from?" He indicated the cheerful flow in the rocky creek bottom.

"Not to be outdone, my grandfather built a diversion line to bring it back. He piped the water into a series of lakes formed by putting rocks and soil across the original creek bed at strategic points. This is the overflow. Since we get forty to fifty inches of rain a year, we have plenty of water for our operations."

"That must have been expensive."

"But worth it." She heard the pride in her voice and laughed ruefully. "One-upmanship over the Carsons has been a rule in my family for as long as I remember."

"Grandchildren often bring families together. Matt and Rose's baby may end the feud."

Susan's spirits perked up. "I can't wait for it to get here. I'm determined to spoil it dreadfully, then tell Rose she isn't raising the baby right. She was always telling me not to be so reckless when I was young."

When they reached one of her favorite spots, a place where the creek cascaded down a series of huge rock slabs, she settled on a convenient boulder in the shade of several mesquites and leaned back on another.

Her thoughts lingered on her sister's coming child, then drifted to the children she would never have. She suddenly missed them, as if they were real and had been taken away.

"I've never thought much about having children," she said, giving voice to her musing. "It was always something in the vague future, sandwiched in between ballet seasons."

"And now?"

She shrugged. "I don't know. It suddenly seems more important than it did. Why do we always want that which is denied to us?"

"Human nature." He leaned back against a tree limb after making sure it didn't contain any thorny surprises. "Since Flynt and Josie married, I find myself thinking more about a family. My friends' lives are changing. I wonder if I should reconsider, too."

"Benedict, the married man," she teased, recalling the Shakespeare play from school days and taking perverse delight in imagining him with maybe five squalling kids, all keeping him awake at night.

He smiled and half closed his eyes.

"What about your family? Are your parents still living?" she asked.

"They both died while I was in my residency. My brother handled all the arrangements."

"You have a brother?" She didn't know why she was surprised by this news. "In Houston?"

"Hawaii. He was stationed there while in the army and married a local girl."

"Do they have children?"

"A daughter. My niece is nineteen—"

"Nineteen?" Susan interrupted in surprise. "He must have married awfully young."

"Not really. Jim's twenty years my senior. We've never been what you might call close. I was a change-of-life surprise for my parents. They were almost fifty when I came along."

"Was that hard, having older parents?"

"The other kids thought it was a little strange, but there were advantages. My parents forgot I was a kid most of the time. They treated me as one of their contemporaries, just a bit shorter and with less gray hair than the rest."

Susan burst into laughter at this humorous picture of his childhood, delivered in a droll voice. "Yes, I can see you and your father puffing on your pipes after dinner, discussing the madness of the younger generation."

"You got it."

His laughter was low and deep, like the river in full spring flow. There was a...richness about him, reminding her of the black loam sometimes found on the bottom land next to the river, where farmers grew their best crops.

She stared at him, at his mouth and the shape of it and thought of the kisses they had shared, at the shiny darkness of his hair and thought of the times she'd run her fingers through it, at the length and breadth of his hands and thought of the caresses he'd bestowed.

With a little start, she realized he was watching her study him. A tiny smile played about the corners of his mouth. She smiled, too, and couldn't look away.

"I've heard of this," he murmured, "but I've never experienced it. Until now."

"Experienced what?"

"This." His gesture took in the two of them.

It was silly to pretend innocence of what he meant. "I know. It's so at odds with my usual..." She couldn't think of a descriptive word. "I really don't have a usual mode of operation with the opposite sex."

"Haven't you ever been involved with your dance partners? I'd have sworn you were in love when I saw you in some doomed love story ballet one time."

She shook her head, then pushed an escaped tendril behind her ear. "All ballerinas fall in love with their first choreographer. Once over that, it's rare for them to become involved. Too much ego, I think."

"Did you fall in love with yours?"

"Yes, but he was seventy and his wife was the company stage director. She stuck pretty close to him."

Michael laughed with her, but he wondered who she might have loved and why they hadn't married. The answer was simple, he realized. Susan was as dedicated to her career as he'd been to his.

In fact, he'd been ruthless during his years and years of training not to get deeply involved. He'd known he'd had too little of himself left to give a woman, much less children. He wouldn't be the kind of absentminded parent to his kids that he'd had as a child.

Not that he hadn't loved his parents. He had. But he'd also known there were other families in which the father tossed a ball to his son, gave him pointers on how to swing a bat and coached the games.

His own father had had a heart condition by the time he came along and had retired by the time he was ten. Which probably explained his interest in medicine and especially in heart surgery.

"Tell me about your childhood. Did you come here often?" he asked.

"Every summer and every holiday. Luckily my mom's parents and sister lived in the county, too, so she visited with them while we kids stayed with my father. We ran back and forth from the ranch to my grandmother's house in those days. I thought it was fun."

"You were a hellion?"

"Well, a daredevil. My brother would taunt his friends for cowardice, then show them that his little sister, a *girl*, would try anything."

She pulled a sprig of mint and rolled it between her palms, producing a cloud of fragrance around them. He liked being in this peaceful place with her. Not that he was entirely relaxed. There was too much awareness between them for that. But it was a good tension, filled with pleasurable anticipation.

He knew they were going to kiss sooner or later.

At the moment, Susan was staring at the cascading water and idly pulling leaves off the mint plant. Her eyes flicked back to him, then away again.

She was still trying to be circumspect, but he wasn't bothering to fight it. Neither of them could take their eyes off each other, and he didn't pretend otherwise.

"I'm going to have to kiss you," he told her, giving fair warning, although he didn't move. Yet.

She heaved a sigh. "I know. It's in your eyes."

"Are you going to resist?" he asked lazily. "A token struggle can add a bit of spice to the moment."

He watched the pulse beating at the side of her neck as her heart sped up. His own had picked up, too. He wanted to make love to her, carefully but thoroughly.

Reaching for her, intending to cuddle her in his lap while they enjoyed their feast of each other, he was surprised when she came to him and, tossing a leg over his thighs, straddled him.

This put their faces on the same level. An equal opportunity position, he realized, and very like the independent little rebel he knew her to be.

"Nice," he whispered.

It was, Susan thought as a mist clouded her thinking. More than nice. Necessary. She had to have more of him.

He wore a long-sleeved shirt, the cuffs rolled up. She unfastened it impatiently and pushed it aside. "Off," she commanded.

Gazing intently into her eyes, he complied, then did the same with her blouse. Her bra followed, then he wrapped her in a tight embrace and brought them together.

She gasped at the wonder of this magical touching. Wine seemed to flow through her veins. "You make me feel sparkly and light inside."

"Like champagne," he agreed, knowing exactly what she meant. "It's the same for me."

"Is it?" She pushed away from him and ran her hands all over his lean, muscular torso. "You have a tan."

"I swim often." He cupped her breasts, liking the way the nipple pushed impudently into his palms, then let his fingers glide down her streamlined body to her thighs. "Your muscles are like steel clad in velvet."

"It's the dancing." Her breath caught when he caressed intimately closer to her body.

Through his slacks, she could feel the rigid length of his erection. Breathing raggedly, she tried to tell herself they should back off from this, that it wasn't wise.

It didn't work.

Leaning close, she rubbed against him. His hand slid between them, finding her most intimate spot. She moaned as pleasure danced up her spine.

Michael took her lips again, holding her head in position with one hand while he explored her through the layers of cloth that separated flesh from flesh.

"Open," he growled.

She opened her lips and let him delve into the sweet heat there. She'd be just as sweet, just as hot, in other places. He knew that, too, and nearly exploded at the thought.

But part of him was monitoring her from moment to moment. He at last drew back and let them breathe. Her face was flushed with passion with no paleness around the mouth.

"Good," he murmured.

"Yes," she panted, rubbing as sensuously as a cat, with no hint of shyness about her hunger for him.

He smiled and gazed into her eyes as he caressed her small, exquisite breasts, giving them both time to come down from the heights a bit.

She smiled back, then writhed against him.

"Vixen," he said on a gasp.

"I need you," she said, loving his heat and the way he caressed her, so urgent and yet so gentle. "You have magic hands." She closed her eyes and let her hands roam over him, learning his body through her touch.

Michael winced. Her words wrung a groan of frustration from him, reminding him of his responsibilities. His hands were a large part of his skill as a surgeon, and he was tentatively her doctor. He caught her roaming hands, now exploring at his waistband.

"Easy," he whispered, although it pained him to stop.

She opened her eyes and watched him, a dreamy invitation in those verdant depths. He noted the rapid rise of her chest, the visible flurry of the pulse in her neck.

"Let me put you on the waiting list," he said, suddenly needing her whole and well. He wanted to make love to her without having to withhold a part of him in order to check her condition.

"What?" Susan couldn't make sense of anything. She didn't want to. The magic, she wanted only that.

"The sooner we get you on the list, the sooner your chances of getting a heart. Before it's too late."

Shock speared through her. He was talking about heart transplant surgery!

Tearing herself out of his arms, she demanded, "Is this how you get your patients to do as you want? You seduce them into agreeing with you?"

He gave her a slow, burning appraisal. "Not usually, but I'm willing to consider whatever works."

Pain—she wasn't sure of its cause—seared her insides. It was a lesson in humility. She'd been thinking only of making love; he'd been thinking of a damned operation.

"No, thanks, Dr. O'Day. I don't mix pleasure with business. Not ever."

Grabbing her clothing, she turned her back and struggled into the bra and shirt, her fingers turning to all thumbs. Finished, she stalked off without once looking back.

Six

After leaving the Wainwright ranch, Michael returned home, did his workout in the pool, then drove to town and picked up an order of barbecue ribs for dinner.

Back at his place, he grabbed a beer from the fridge, intending to sit on the patio with its view of Lake Maria to the north and Mission Creek to the south and enjoy his meal.

No such luck.

"Hello, Doc," a gravelly voice said as soon as he stepped outside.

Michael turned to see the same two henchmen of Carmine Mercado's who had visited him once before. "Hey," he said quite jovially, but with an inward grimace. "If I'd known you were coming, I'd have ordered more ribs. Care for a beer?"

"No," the older mobster spoke before the younger one could open his mouth.

Michael had to give the man credit—he was all business. "What's on your mind?" He settled at the patio table and indicated they were welcome to take a seat.

They remained standing. "I have a new proposition for you," Carmine's spokesman told him.

Michael took a swig of beer, ignoring the tantalizing aroma coming from the container of ribs, slaw, jalapeño peppers and corn bread. "What's that?"

For the first time, the man looked a bit uncomfortable. "We supply the heart. You get the hospital to agrec to let you do the surgery."

"On Carmine Mercado," Michael said, not bothering to hide the sardonic tone.

"Yeah."

"Who's volunteered to supply the heart?"

The younger man grinned. The older one didn't. "You don't have to concern yourself with that part."

"You recall there has to be a match—"

"There will be."

The black market, Michael concluded. There was a huge international black market in human organs as well as those of animals, all used for everything that one could imagine. And quite a few that a person probably wouldn't think of. People were a strange and macabre lot, taken as a whole.

However, this was no time to wax philosophical, he reminded himself. His guests awaited an answer.

"I'll see what I can do. Please pass the word that six blood factors *have* to match before there's a prayer of success. Six. Got that?"

Both men nodded.

"Have your boss's health records sent to my office in Houston. I'll look them over next week. Then he'll have to come in for blood work and a thorough examination. After that, I'll let him know what his chances are.''

The older man frowned, then nodded again.

Without another word, they walked off the patio, around his house and disappeared. He heard an engine start up a few seconds later from farther down the street.

With a sigh of part exasperation, part amusement, part worry, he wondered what the hell he should do now. Call the police? The FBI? The CIA? Who the devil handled a case like this?

And what was he to report?

That some thugs might bring a heart to him to be inserted in their boss, assuming they found one that matched Mercado's need?

Man, what a farce this was turning out to be. He gave a snort of laughter. His peaceful existence in the middle of Texas's ranching belt had ceased, hmm, when?

Ah, the day he'd nearly run down Susan Wainwright, prima ballerina, stubborn hellion and all woman.

Hunger attacked him, in the stomach and lower. He opened the styrene box. His stomach he could accommodate. The other hunger would have to wait.

Sunday, after the usual golf game in which Tyler whipped them all again, Michael went to the temporary structure housing the Men's Grill. He ordered a cheeseburger and fries for lunch, then added a salad as a bow to good nutrition to appease his conscience.

Spence Harrison, the D.A. and their usual golfing partner, joined him while Flynt raced home to be with his wife. He ordered the same.

Michael noticed their waitress was Daisy again. The gal seemed to work all the time.

"Spence, old man, I got a slight problem," Michael said as soon as they were alone.

"Speak, son. I'll give you the benefit of my vast wisdom and experience."

"There're these two guys who have visited me twice now. They, uh, seem to be able to enter my home at will."

The humor left Spence's eyes. "You don't say. What do they want?"

"That's the odd thing. At first I assumed it was a robbery, but no such luck. They want me to operate on Carmine Mercado."

Spence straightened from his relaxed, somewhat indolent posture. "What?"

"Yeah, it kinda surprised me, too. I told them it wasn't up to me, but to the hospital board."

"Of which you're a part."

"I didn't mention that." Michael glanced around to make sure no one seemed to be listening. He'd chosen a table a little apart from the others in the grill. Fortunately, it was early for the usual lunch crowd to arrive, and, except for two elderly men, they had the place to themselves.

"They're bound to find out," Spence said.

"Probably. Last night they told me they could supply the heart. All I have to do is take care of convincing the hospital to allow the surgery."

Spence's eyebrows shot up. "I see."

"What do I do now, O great wise one?"

"I was afraid you were going to ask." Spence propped his chin in his hand and thought. "We can't arrest anyone for a possible crime. Unless we can catch them red-handed with the victim, we don't have much of a chance at establishing a case."

"I suspect they've put out feelers on the black market for an organ donor."

"It's a big market and growing," Spence muttered. "With every advance in science, police work gets both tougher and easier—tougher because the crooks use it to their advantage, easier because we do, too, with DNA testing and all that."

"I don't want to hear about your problems. I want a solution to mine," Michael reminded his friend.

"String him along. Tell him you're talking to the other members of the hospital board to see how they feel before making a formal request."

"Right. I already said Mercado would have to

come in for an extensive exam and blood work before I could even consider his chances.''

Spence stretched and yawned. ''Okay then, we got your problem solved.''

''Temporarily. I don't think the Texas Mafia don is an easy man to put off for very long.''

''Maybe we'll nail him for Carl Bridges's murder before you have to act.''

Michael was at once interested. ''You think so?''

''Hell, no. I'm just daydreaming aloud. The bosses keep their hands clean, so the Feds will have to nail Mercado for income tax evasion or some crap like that. Keep me informed of your dealings with him, though. Just in case.''

''Will do.'' Michael exchanged rueful glances with his friend and wondered what had drawn Spence into his line of work. After their salads arrived and the blonde was gone, he asked the attorney about it.

''Funny you should ask. I was thinking of that very thing last night,'' Spence admitted, his brown eyes taking on an introspective light.

The D.A. was around Michael's age. At six feet, he was a couple of inches shorter, but was as lean and hard muscled.

Spence kept himself in shape, Michael noted with his doctor's eye. That was good. He needed physical outlets to handle the stress of his job, dealing with criminals and courts and the extremely slow wheels of justice.

"I don't recall if I told you, but Flynt, Luke, Tyler and I were charged with manslaughter years ago."

"I've heard the story."

"Carl Bridges was the attorney who defended us. That was a life-changing experience for me. I decided, if we made it, I was going to go into law and help people." Spence clenched one fist and banged it on the table. "I'd give my right arm to put away the goons who killed Carl."

A tray landed on their table with a crash that reverberated through the room. Daisy, their waitress, turned her back to them and put her hands over her face.

Michael jumped to his feet. "Hey, you okay?"

Pulling her hands down, he quickly examined her face but saw no signs of an imminent fainting spell.

"I'm fine." She pulled away and rubbed one eye. "It was just…I got something in my eye."

"Something in my eye" sounded like "somethin' in mah ahh," when spoken in her twang.

"Let me see," he offered, picking up a napkin from the table.

"No. It's fine now." She blinked several times to show him. "Please, Dr. O'Day, be seated. Your food is getting cold. The manager will have my hide if it's sent back."

Michael consented to take his seat and let her

serve the meal. She topped off their iced tea glasses, checked that they had everything and left. He watched her hurried stride as she disappeared toward the kitchen.

Spence studied Michael. "What?" he finally asked after taking a bite of his cheeseburger.

"She had tears in both eyes," Michael said. "Usually, when you get something in your eye, only the one waters, not both, at least, not copiously. Daisy was about to burst into a storm of weeping."

"Probably a fight with her boyfriend," Spence suggested, shrugging the woman's worries aside.

Michael resumed the previous conversation. "Any info you can share on Carl's death?"

Spence shook his head. He sighed. "Last night I dreamed of Haley Mercado."

"The girl whose drowning you four were charged with?"

"Yes. I was in love with her all through school. I think we all were. At the time of her death, she was engaged to Frank Del Brio."

Michael knew Del Brio was a big man with the mob and that the drowned girl's uncle was Carmine Mercado. Her father and brother were also involved in racketeering.

"Who will take Carmine's place when he goes?" Michael asked, curious about the workings of the Mafia.

Spence grimaced. "Whoever carries the biggest

stick. Some are betting on Del Brio, but Ricky is the logical heir. He's tougher than his old man, Johnny, and sharper.''

Michael caught the disheartened note in his friend's tone. ''Ricky Mercado was a school chum?''

''Yeah. We were all real friends at one time—me, Flynt, Tyler, Luke and Ricky. We did everything together, including the Gulf War.'' Spence sighed. ''It was the celebration upon making it home that led to Haley's death. Ricky and his family hated us after that.''

''A tough break,'' Michael said in sincere sympathy.

''The irony is that Ricky and his family wanted me behind bars then. Now I want to see them there.'' He muttered a curse, his eyes dark and filled with painful memories.

Michael saw Frank Del Brio come out of the main lobby and stand on the sidewalk, gazing toward the golf course. A chill, like a cold hand from a grave, crept along his neck. There was something about the don's right-hand man that he didn't like.

''The police didn't find a body at first,'' Spence continued. ''They dragged the lake and finally found it near the base of the dam a couple of weeks later. It was Haley, they decided. Who else could it be? But the odd thing was that her dental records had been lost, so they couldn't compare them for a positive identification.''

When Spence lapsed into silence, Michael ate without speaking, too, giving the other man time to get over the past before turning to a lighter subject. "I hope somebody beats Tyler soon. He's getting a big head from winning all the time."

"Not to mention wiping out my lunch money every week," Spence said with a wry laugh.

Across the way, Michael spied Frank Del Brio watching them. There was something unnerving about the guy. He studied a person with the impassive expression of a snake looking over a handy supply of eggs in a robin's nest. For a second, his eyes met Michael's before moving on.

Frank Del Brio viewed the D.A. and his doctor friend through an icy rage. The little scene with the blonde had been touching. Just what, he wondered, had upset her.

Something Spence Harrison and the hotshot surgeon who was going to operate on Carmine had been saying? How much gossip and speculation did she overhear as she worked silently and efficiently in the grill and café? How much truth and how many secrets were disclosed within her hearing? Enough that he should worry?

"Hey, Frank, you think that snooty doc will fix Carmine up?" the younger man of the two with him asked.

Not if he had anything to say about it.

Frank didn't voice that opinion to the two enforcers. "Sure. Why not? Carmine's insurance is paid up," he said, drawing a grin from the younger man and a wary eye from the older one.

Frank shifted uneasily under that gaze. These men reported directly to Carmine. The older of the two had been around a long time and was loyal to the don.

So was he. For now.

But he wasn't going to wait around forever for the old man to die. Carmine had already had a long and useful life. It was time to turn the reins over to a younger man. He meant to see that younger man was himself and not the old man's nephew, Ricky Mercado.

Eyeing Spence and the doctor, he wondered about progress in the Bridges murder. Also the case involving the baby found here at the country club.

He'd seen the passport of the baby while he was cleaning up evidence left by Alex Black at the home of Carl Bridges. The photo had disclosed dark hair and eyes with golden flecks in the brown. Johnny Mercado and his son, Ricky, had eyes like those. Also their daughter, who'd been his fiancée.

Haley was supposed to have drowned years ago. He'd believed that until a mysterious nun had showed up at Isadora Mercado's hospital bedside. The guard Carmine had placed at the door said he'd overheard the nun tell Isadora that she was her daughter.

A touching family reunion, no doubt.

He wanted another one. Just him and Haley. He had a few questions that needed answers from the woman who would rather have staged her own death than marry him.

Had she gone to another man? It hadn't been Flynt, Tyler, Luke or Spence, the four bosom buddies of his rival, Ricky Mercado. However, someone had helped her escape him and their coming marriage. Carl Bridges? Most likely.

Ah. An idea dawned as bright as a summer morning. If the foundling were in his care instead of Flynt Carson's, would the elusive Haley come out of hiding?

The fury rose. He soothed it until he could once again think in the frigid clarity of total logic, without emotion.

A few minutes later, smiling slyly, he decided it was time the whole Mercado clan learned a lesson about thwarting Frank Del Brio. They thought he was ruthless, but they didn't yet know what ruthless meant. They would learn.

"I'm off," Spence said. "Sunday isn't a rest day for me like for the rest of you bums. I have reports to read."

"See ya," Michael said as his friend left the restaurant. Suppressing a yawn, he thought about his afternoon—he'd go home, take a nap, get his laps in, then...

He tried to think of something exciting, but only Susan came to mind. Yeah, he knew what he'd like to do in that department. She'd got under his skin, way under. In more ways than he could count.

Thinking about her conjured up an image. No, not just an image. She was here in person, walking toward the diving pool with the jock he'd seen at her table last weekend. Inside, something hot and jealous arose.

Hey, she isn't yours, he reminded the stubborn streak that thought she was, or should be.

While he watched, Susan and her friend entered the gate to the pool. Laughing at some no doubt lame joke, she tossed a robe and towel onto a chair, then headed for the high dive. Michael's heart thundered. Leaping to his feet, he ran across the lawn and garden toward the diving area at a dead run. No use in yelling at her. There wasn't a prayer she could hear him above the shrieks from the children's pool, which was close by.

She did a neat swan dive into the cool waters just as he reached the gate.

He raced inside, kicked off his shoes, tossed his wallet onto the concrete and did a running dive from the side.

"Hey!" the lifeguard yelled.

Michael dove to the center bottom where the suction from the pool filtering pump was pulling at Susan's feebly struggling body. Slipping an arm around her waist, he kicked toward the surface.

Their heads broke the water just as the lifeguard shouted into a bullhorn, "You, sir, remove yourself from the pool immediately!"

Michael refrained from telling the young man where he could go. He hauled Susan over to the side. "Here, take her. She's in a faint."

"I'm not," she denied, but so breathlessly weak his heart contracted in pity.

The lifeguard, fear suddenly on his face, lifted Susan from the water while Michael hauled himself onto the side.

"Lay her down," he ordered, then bent over her supine figure and checked the pulse at her neck. "Too fast," he muttered. "You're missing too many beats."

"What…happened?" she asked, still gasping.

He scowled at her. "You went from hot to cold in an instant, from less pressure to greater. Your body couldn't handle the demands of the sudden changes. When are you going to stop this childish behavior?"

"Who the hell do you think you are to talk to her this way?" her date the jerk demanded.

"Her heart doctor," Michael answered in a snarl. "She can't do this kind of thing anymore."

"Her heart— What kind of thing?" the younger man spluttered. "What are you talking about?"

"Her life," Michael said, looking into her eyes. "Her death," he added only for her ears.

She sighed and closed her eyes.

Michael sent a visual challenge to the jerk. "I'm taking her home. Now."

The guy spread his hands in surrender and stepped back out of way when Michael lifted Susan. "Get her things," he ordered. "And mine."

The man silently did as he was told, helping get Susan and their things stored in Michael's car. "Let me know if there's anything I can do," he said, after closing the car door and stopping by the driver's side.

"Thanks. I can handle it."

The younger man, subdued and worried, waved them off. Michael decided the guy might not be so bad after all.

Once at his house, Michael wondered if he should have taken her to her home rather than his. But he knew he wasn't going to. Not unless she requested it.

Ignoring her frown, he carried her to the patio, wrapped the terry robe around her shoulders and got them each a glass of raspberry tea before going to his room to change. He returned and sat in a cushioned chair with a sigh.

"I ruined your day," she said, "not to mention your clothing. Send me the dry-cleaning bill."

"Thanks, but they're washable. The housekeeper will take care of it." He studied her face. "How do you feel?"

"The way anyone would who made a spectacle of herself. Like an idiot."

Seeing her humor assert itself, he relaxed and took a long drink of the fruit-flavored tea. "Well," he said agreeably, "you should."

She burst into laughter. "Please don't be polite. Just say whatever you think."

He grinned.

She looked into his eyes. The laughter died way. His grin faded. He gazed into her eyes and saw everything he'd ever wanted, just an arm's length away.

Seven

"Did you happen to bring my bag?" Susan asked. "I'd like to change clothes."

She pretended not to notice his dexterous fingers as they brushed along her forearm. Grabbing the glass of tea as an excuse to move away from him, she took a big drink, choked, coughed, then managed a smile.

"In the car," he said. "I'll get it."

When he was gone, she sighed and laid her head back, her eyes closed. She was suddenly, unaccountably weary and mentally tired. Tired of fighting. Tired of being cool and in control. Tired of denying what she felt around this man. She wanted to quit worrying and simply live.

"Here you go."

She looked at him, this tall man with magic hands, blue eyes and a beautiful smile. Taking a slow, calming breath, she stood. "Where can I change?"

"This way."

Following at his heels, she observed the house as they walked through it. The living room was huge, with a vaulted ceiling, the wall facing the patio filled with windows. The entryway, kitchen and a den with pocket doors flowed around it in an open floor plan made for entertaining.

The floors were polished natural stone tiles throughout, in colors ranging from tan to golden beige to pale brick-red. Inlaid oak strips outlined an Oriental rug, which in turn defined a seating arrangement in front of a fireplace faced with blue-hued stone interspersed with the tan and beige. There wasn't any other furniture.

Going down the hallway, she noted a library off to the left, a bedroom to the right. Neither had furniture. A second door to the right disclosed a bathroom. He indicated she should enter the third door to the right.

At the end of the corridor, she noticed double doors, both open. Inside them, she spotted the master suite that spanned the width of the house on that end. She got a glimpse of a broad bed and shades of blue and tan.

"Would you like the ten-cent tour?" he asked.

Startled, she realized she'd been standing there, staring at his bedroom and thinking about…things.

"Uh, no. I'd better change." But still she paused. "You haven't furnished your home here."

He glanced at the empty room across the hall. "I'll let my wife do that. When I acquire one."

"You sound as if you'll order a bride from a catalog. When you get ready to acquire one," she added, mocking his choice of words. "What if you fall madly in love before you're ready for the acquisition?"

His expression changed, becoming more guarded. "I expect love will grow from mutual interests and respect, much like my parents shared."

She thought of her parents and the divorce that had taken place before she'd ever known of days when they'd been one family unit, supposedly happy. Suddenly, although she hadn't lived much during that time, she missed it.

Once, she'd believed passionate attraction was the beginning of true commitment. Michael obviously didn't. Depression darkened her spirits. Around this man, her emotions seemed to go awry.

"I thought attraction was the first key to romance and perhaps a lasting love," she said, a question in her voice.

His eyes probed hers. "I admit there are feelings between a male and female, very intense ones. To put it bluntly, attraction usually starts from passion, which is a sexual need that has nothing to do with love."

"I don't think there can be great passion without great feelings. Sex is a natural part of any attraction, but so is love." Until that moment, she hadn't realized she felt so strongly on the subject.

His smile was fleeting. "You're a romantic," he accused softly, a seriousness about him that intrigued

GET 2

HOW TO GET YOUR
2 FREE BOOKS AND FREE GIFT!

1. Peel off the MIRA sticker on the front cover. Place it in the space provided at right. This automatically entitles you to receive two free books and an exciting surprise gift.

2. Send back this card and you'll get 2 "The Best of the Best™" novels. These books have a combined cover price of $11.98 or more in the U.S. and $13.98 or more in Canada, but they are yours to keep absolutely FREE!

3. There's <u>no</u> catch. You're under <u>no</u> obligation to buy anything. We charge nothing – ZERO – for your first shipment. And you don't have to make any minimum number of purchases – not even one!

4. We call this line "The Best of the Best" because each month you'll receive the best books by some of today's most popular authors. These authors show up time and time again on all the major bestseller lists and their books sell out as soon as they hit the stores. You'll like the convenience of getting them delivered to your home at our special discount prices . . . and you'll love your *Heart to Heart* subscriber newsletter featuring author news, horoscopes, recipes, book reviews and much more!

5. We hope that after receiving your free books you'll want to remain a subscriber. But the choice is yours – to continue or cancel, anytime at all! So why not take us up on our invitation, with no risk of any kind. You'll be glad you did!

6. And remember…we'll send you a surprise gift ABSOLUTELY FREE just for giving "The Best of the Best" a try.

SPECIAL FREE GIFT!

We'll send you a fabulous surprise gift, absolutely FREE, simply for accepting our no-risk offer!

Visit us online at www.mirabooks.com

® and TM are trademarks of Harlequin Enterprises Limited.

BOOKS FREE!

Hurry!

Return this card promptly to GET 2 FREE BOOKS & A FREE GIFT!

The Best of the Best™

Affix
peel-off
MIRA
sticker here

YES! Please send me the 2 FREE "The Best of the Best" novels and FREE gift for which I qualify. I understand that I am under no obligation to purchase anything further, as explained on the back and on the opposite page.

385 MDL DNHR   185 MDL DNHS

FIRST NAME   LAST NAME

ADDRESS

APT.#   CITY

STATE/PROV.   ZIP/POSTAL CODE

Offer limited to one per household and not valid to current subscribers of "The Best of the Best." All orders subject to approval. Books received may vary.

The Best of the Best™ — Here's How it Works:

Accepting your 2 free books and gift places you under no obligation to buy anything. You may keep the books and gift and return the shipping statement marked "cancel." If you do not cancel, about a month later we will send you 4 additional novels and bill you just $4.49 each in the U.S., or $4.99 each in Canada, plus 25¢ shipping & handling per book and applicable taxes if any.* That's the complete price and — compared to cover prices of $5.99 or more each in the U.S. and $6.99 or more each in Canada — it's quite a bargain! You may cancel at any time, but if you choose to continue, every month we'll send you 4 more books, which you may either purchase at the discount price or return to us and cancel your subscription.

*Terms and prices subject to change without notice. Sales tax applicable in N.Y. Canadian residents will be charged applicable provincial taxes and GST.

If offer card is missing write to: The Best of the Best, 3010 Walden Ave., P.O. Box 1867, Buffalo, NY 14240-1867

BUSINESS REPLY MAIL
FIRST-CLASS MAIL   PERMIT NO. 717-003   BUFFALO, NY

POSTAGE WILL BE PAID BY ADDRESSEE

THE BEST OF THE BEST
3010 WALDEN AVE
PO BOX 1867
BUFFALO NY 14240-9952

NO POSTAGE
NECESSARY
IF MAILED
IN THE
UNITED STATES

and alarmed her. "But then, your life has been built around romantic fairy tales. *Romeo and Juliet. Swan Lake.* Why are they all tragedies?"

"Not all. Some end happily." Not sure where this was going, she wondered what had ever induced her to broach the subject. "I'll only be a second," she said, taking her bag from him and practically running into the guest bedroom.

"The bathroom connects to this bedroom, if you want to take a shower. Warm water, not hot," he advised. "Yell if you need anything."

If she felt faint, she interpreted his statement, resentment rising at her physical condition. "It isn't fair," she muttered.

"It isn't," he agreed, understanding in his eyes, "but it's the way life is. Some people get lemons and make lemonade."

He hooked a finger under her chin and peered into her eyes. She flashed him a sarcastic smile. "So get over it and get on with it?" she asked.

"Maybe it's time for you to try a new course," he suggested softly. "Maybe that's what your heart is telling you. I believe in listening to the body's messages."

For a second she was swept into a maelstrom of nope and a vision of a future that encompassed... what?

Home? Husband? Children?

Teaching? Gardening? Sewing?

For an awful second, she thought she would burst into tears. "I think I will take a shower, if you don't mind."

His eyes darkened. "Not at all."

Carrying the straw beach bag, she went into the room and closed the door. Here, the bedroom furniture was minimal—a single bed, a bureau, a small, rickety table with a mirror mounted on the wall over it.

The bathroom made up in elegance what the bedroom lacked, though. It was tiled with pink marble. No, granite, she realized as she peeled out of her swimsuit and robe and stepped into the huge tubshower combination.

The granite covered the floor, walls and ceiling, making the room a beautiful grotto. Real ferns grew in brass pots beside a window.

The faucets were brass, flat and three inches wide so that the water cascaded from it in a waterfall. The showerheads, one at each end, were the same, but each had a regular spray attachment connected.

The tub was formed of the pink granite with tiny black flecks embedded in it. The twin sinks were black porcelain, as was the toilet, tucked into its own alcove.

Very stylish.

Seeing a brush and comb on the counter, she wondered who stayed here with him, then recalled he had a niece.

Not that she cared in the least.

Liar.

She found she did care, and it wasn't a good feeling. Jealousy wasn't something she recalled ever experiencing.

With a deep sigh, she washed and rinsed, then dried off on a pink bath sheet. Dressed in a shorts and T-shirt outfit, wearing her favorite espadrilles, she quickly dried her hair, put on lipstick and went to find her host.

"I'm ready to go home," she announced, finding him on the patio again.

"I think we need to talk."

"I'd rather not." In those moments of weakness and panic at the pool, she'd decided to accede, but now she felt much better, her old self, really. The fear had gone.

He indicated the chair. "I poured you a fresh glass of tea. Sit a spell and relax," he invited.

"I think I'd better go home. I've been taking a nap in the afternoon of late, on your advice to take it easy."

"Good. The chairs recline. I usually take a nap out here myself. It's warm enough."

She found she didn't really want to leave. Tension hummed along her nerves. She'd been lying again. It wasn't a nap that interested her. She wanted to stay…with him.

Dropping her bag by the patio door, she joined

him. "Your view is wonderful. I didn't realize you could see so far from here."

"The ridge is over fifty feet high. Around here, that's a mountain."

His laughter flowed over her, deep and melodious, causing vibrations that disappeared into some hidden place inside her. She laughed, too.

For the moment, she felt young and happy and foolish. And she didn't care. If he touched her again, she wasn't going to run like a frightened antelope.

"You want a bowl of ice cream?" he asked.

She lazily shook her head and lowered the back of the chair down a couple of notches. While he went to the kitchen, she surveyed the land spread out before her like a tabletop, rolling and rougher to the west, but flat toward the east.

On Lake Maria, she could make out small sailing prams, powerboats pulling water-skiers and the marina on the distant shore. Over there was a swimming area and a place visitors could rent paddleboats and fishing dories.

From the larger lake, Mission Creek coursed merrily down to the dam put in by the town fathers, where it formed a small recreation lake and also supplied the area's drinking water. This dam had cut off the supply of water to the Wainwright ranch, but a pipeline had restored it.

All's well that ends well, she reminded herself. Except it hadn't. The Carsons and her family were still enemies, her sister had married a Carson, and *she* was in the home of a man known to be friends with the Carsons.

Restlessness, of an unknown cause, poured over her like a sudden rain shower out of a clear sky that they sometimes got in the summer. She gazed moodily at the landscape again.

It was midafternoon now. The sun was drifting toward the west, casting longer and longer shadows on the grass under the mesquites and oaks east of the house. Pines dotted the slopes of the rolling hills and ridges on this side of the wide tableland.

Home.

She'd missed it. All the years she'd lived in Houston hadn't erased her ties to this land, this place where her ancestors had forged their homesteads.

Michael returned. Her heart sped up a bit. Smiling, she acknowledged the attraction. It had been a long time since she'd felt this kind of tension around a man.

"Bite?" he asked.

The cold spoon touched her lips. Opening her mouth, she met his gaze as she accepted the treat. He'd made a sundae with sliced bananas, pecans and fudge sauce over the ice cream. It was delicious. They practically licked the bowl.

"You have a sweet tooth," she told him.

He admitted it with a nod. "Ice cream is my downfall. When I was a kid, we had a neighbor who made the best homemade ice cream and fudge sauce I ever ate. She used to let me lick the pan after she poured the sauce. I've been hooked ever since.''

She envisioned him as a tall, lanky boy, one mostly ignored by his well-meaning older parents, but whose neighbor let him be a kid. It was a nice image.

"I'm surprised you Texans don't put jalapeños in your ice cream. I've found it in everything else— pizzas, beans, slaw, corn bread. I had to get used to eating hot peppers in self-defense,'' he complained.

"You weren't born in Houston?'' For some reason, she'd assumed he was a native.

"No. Tennessee. Both my parents taught at a university there. I did my internship in Houston and decided to stay. There was nothing to go back home for.''

Although he spoke cheerfully, she detected loneliness behind the tone. It touched a chord in her, echoing her feeling of isolation of late. Rolling her head to the side, she studied him.

His blue eyes were framed in dark lashes that matched the black of his hair. His eyes and bright smile contrasted nicely with the tan of his face, caused, she knew, by rounds of golf with his friends and the swimming workouts he'd mentioned.

Rose said Matt and Flynt considered Michael an all-around good guy. Thinking of the dinner with the Carson brothers and their wives, she thought of how it could be if she and Michael were a couple, if they married and settled here.

"What are you thinking?" he asked suddenly.

"About us," she said truthfully.

He closed his eyes and muttered, "Damnation," then he stood, bent and scooped her into his arms.

The next thing she knew she was ensconced in his lap, both of them in his chair. It felt perfectly natural. She slipped one arm behind his neck, the other across his chest and laid her head on his shoulder. Better.

For a long time they sat there like that, then he combed his fingers through her hair, toyed with a strand for a while, then ran his palm along her shoulder and arm.

"I love the way you feel," he murmured, resting his cheek on her temple. "Strong and supple and smooth."

"You're the same."

"But not as soft," he contradicted with a laugh.

"Hairier," she added, and ran a hand under his polo shirt and gave a little tug.

He caught her hand, pulled it free and kissed the palm, then lingered to run his lips along each knuckle. His chest pressed hers as he inhaled then exhaled sharply.

She was aware of his hunger and her own, of the tension that spiraled around them in silken threads of longing. She wondered how much of herself she was willing to share with this man.

For a second, worry arose at the thought of a serious involvement, then it simply vanished. At this moment, it just didn't matter.

"If I have the operation," she began, then stopped. She tilted her head back on his arm. "Some people don't make it through surgery."

His eyes met hers, open and candid and honest. He didn't deny the possibility she'd been about to voice—that *she* might not make it.

Taking a deep breath, she faced that possibility and the fact that she didn't want to die before knowing passion with him. If it was the last thing she ever had, then she wanted to grab it with both hands.

"I want to make love," she said. "With you."

He stroked her cheek with his long, supple fingers. "It's an idea I've been mulling over for the past eight days."

"Since last Saturday when you nearly ran over me?" she teased, striving for a light note when she felt so sad deep inside, as if this truly was the end.

"Yes."

"It seems longer, doesn't it?"

"Sometimes people can share a lot in a short time. That makes it seem a lifetime."

"It could be for me."

He laid a finger over her lips. "Not with me as your doctor. I won't allow you to die."

She believed him. At that moment, she did.

When he rose with her still in his arms, she clasped him around the shoulders. In his room, he let her slide down until her feet touched the floor. With one sweep, he tossed the comforter to the end of the bed.

"We won't need these," he murmured, and peeled off his shirt. He helped her undress, taking turns until they were both breathless by the time he finished.

Sliding an arm around her back and thighs, he lifted her onto the king-size bed and settled beside her. Tremors raced over her skin as he perused her from head to toe.

"Very nice," he said. "Very much as I've envisioned every night this past week. Days, too."

She rubbed her fingertips over his chest. "Yes. It's madness, but I've had dreams of us like this."

He pressed her against the pillow and strung kisses like hot pearls along the valley between her breasts. "We're going to take this very slowly."

"I'm not sure I can handle slow."

"I'll do it for you. We'll build to a point, then we'll rest. Then we'll start all over, but at a higher level each time until we reach the final peak. I've planned the details over and over this past week."

Between every word, he kissed her at a different point, working downward, slowly, so slowly. She breathed deeply and let the sensation grow, slowly, as he said.

She gasped when he circled her belly button with his tongue. "I didn't know...I had so many sensitive spots."

He raised his head and delved deeply into her eyes. "There's more. Fair warning—I intend to find them all."

Tugging at his hair, she brought his face to hers and kissed him with the wild longing that ached to burst free from someplace inside where it had lain dormant all these years.

"Michael," she whispered, desperate to tell him of the ache inside, of the passionate ache for more.

"I know, love. We'll get there. It'll be the sweetest journey either of us ever took."

He began again, starting at the hollow of her throat and working his way to each breast, then skimming over her rib cage to her abdomen, past her groin and along each thigh.

His intimate exploration touched off an earthquake that caused fierce tremors all through her.

"Easy," Michael whispered, then went back to his task, one that brought him more pleasure than he'd ever known. He wanted to make every moment the best she'd ever known, too.

But he would do it carefully, aware of all her physical needs and the demands on her heart. He found this didn't diminish his own anticipation in the least. On the contrary, every caress was heightened to its fullest.

Susan couldn't control the little cries that escaped her as his touch became more exciting, driving her to ecstasy and beyond. "Come to me," she said, a plea and a demand.

"Not yet. There's lots more I want us to share. We're not going to rush it."

His voice was deep, dark and husky. It filled her soul with light and music, like moonlight on rushing water. From the darkness was born a brilliance, a single flare of intense light. She knew the light was this man who kissed her so passionately, so tenderly.

"You make me weep," she told him, panting as he lifted her higher and higher with his magic. "Your touch is so beautiful, it fills me to overflowing."

"Do whatever feels good," he urged with laughter and desire equally mingled in the words.

When she could no longer breathe, when air was no longer necessary for her existence, he gently stroked his hands over her and returned to her mouth, letting the tension drain slowly.

She clasped his hard phallus between her thighs and pressed close. "I want you. I've never wanted anyone like this...so fierce...so hurting in its intensity."

"I know. Be still now and rest. There's more. I promise we'll have it all."

Resting against his warmth, she experienced a peace she'd never known to go with the incredible passion he stirred in her. She gazed at him, questioning why this should be so.

"Why?" she asked him. "Why you? Why me?"

"We strike sparks off each other." He took her mouth in a kiss that burned all thoughts to cinders.

As he promised, he took her nearer and nearer the peak, but without letting her go over. At one point, she took his bottom lip between her teeth and demanded that he come to her. "Now!"

His gaze, hot with desire, lazy with laughter, roamed over her as he, too, panted with the effort to hold back. "I like a woman who knows what she wants."

Michael knew he was near the point of no return. Pinning her arms to the mattress so that she couldn't touch him and take him too far, too fast, he moved down her body and this time he didn't stop.

When she went over the edge with a little scream, he let her rest, then he rose and, after securing protection, entered her. Then he started building again, letting both of them ride the crest, higher and faster this time.

Susan writhed uncontrollably. The intensity was so great, the world collapsed to this instant, this wild joining of body and spirit. She was consumed. And so was he. They went as one to the sensual paradise she'd dreamed of.

"The best," he whispered, kissing her temple.

She couldn't speak. Spent, she could only lie

against his strength in complete wonder. As she slowly recovered, a fear began to grow in her.

Was she... Could she be... Had she fallen in love with the famous surgeon?

As if reading her mind, he raised on an elbow and gazed down at her solemnly. "I think I've done what no doctor is supposed to do."

"Make love to a patient?"

He shook his head and didn't smile in response to her playful tone. "Fall in love with one."

The world stopped spinning, but her mind whirled. "You can't. It's against the rules."

"There are no rules where you're concerned." He stroked a sheen of perspiration from between her breasts. "By the time I knew of your condition, it was too late."

"It was the same for me," she admitted.

His eyes narrowed at he stared down at her, then his beautiful smile bloomed across his face. "I've never mentioned love to a woman before."

Happiness bubbled inside her. "It's kind of scary. I've always been so focused on my career."

"Same here. This opens up a world of possibilities." He laid his hand over her heart, which still beat too fast, too irregularly. "Let me operate."

"Don't push. Please," she begged, "not now."

"All right, but I'm not going to give you up. I want more than a few months."

The future came rushing at her, vague and uncertain. She closed her mind against it. "Let's just have *this* for now." She caressed along his sides and hips.

"For now," he agreed.

But she saw the determination in his eyes. She wanted time with him, she realized. A lifetime. For her, that was three to twelve months. Unless she had surgery.

Invalid.

When her primary physician had first mentioned the heart replacement, she'd done some research. A nurse friend had told her she'd have to take around ninety pills a day. A day! And stay mostly isolated from all but immediate family for months afterward. Everyone would have to scrub and wear a surgical gown before they could visit her.

It came to her that Michael was used to doing that. He would be there for her throughout the ordeal.

As a doctor or a lover?

"Can you be both?" she asked. "Can you be my doctor and my lover?"

"Yes."

His confidence increased her uncertainty. Would she be a whole person after the operation? Would she be able to function as a wife or a mother?

"Think about it," he murmured, then bent to kiss her. "But not at this moment."

Her heart did a flip at the look in his eyes. Was this love or mere madness? If love, then what? She hadn't a clue as to what was best for either of them.

The phone rang before things got too heated. Michael answered, listened intently, asked a few questions, then hung up. "I have to go. A heart has become available."

"In Houston?"

"Yes. A car accident. The man had a signed organ donor card on him." He headed for the shower, then paused. "Take my car to get home. I'll call you when I return, okay?"

"I can't drive."

He'd forgotten. "I'll ask Chuck to take you. Do you have a private number, or should I call the ranch when I get back?"

"The ranch. I'll give you my mother's number, too."

Thirty minutes later, ready to take off, he placed his hands on her shoulders. "I want to put you on the list."

"Let me think about it, just until you get back."

He nodded. There was nothing he could do at the present. "Take care," he murmured, and brushed a kiss over her lips. He wanted more, but with Chuck standing by, he contented himself with a taste. There would be more when he returned to Mission Ridge.

"Thanks for your help," he said to Chuck after they'd pushed the plane onto the tarmac.

"No sweat, man."

They shook hands. Michael climbed into the plane

and took off for Houston. For the next few hours, his life was on hold while he performed lifesaving surgery on another.

Susan waited until the plane was out of sight, then she turned to Chuck with a smile. "Ready?"

"Yep."

He drove her to the ranch in the sleek sports car. "You ought to marry the doc," he advised. "He needs someone to come home to."

Her laugh was a bit shaky. "I don't know. It's a big step. What about you? Is marriage on your horizon?"

"Well, there is this sweet little gal, works as a waitress at Coyote Harry's."

"I've eaten there. They have the best fajitas in the state of Texas. Are you two engaged?" She found she had an avid interest in other people's relationships all of a sudden.

Chuck grinned and came to a stop in front of the ranch house. "I'm thinking of popping the question, but she's pretty skittish. Her first husband was a jerk."

Susan opened the door and hopped out. "Good luck. Thanks for the ride." She waved as Chuck drove around the semicircle driveway and headed back to Mission Ridge.

She found her home deserted. She didn't know where her father was. Esperanza and her family were probably at their house. There was a casserole in the oven and a salad in the fridge for supper. Susan helped herself, then went outside.

A stroll along the creek to her favorite place would help clear her head. She had to think about Michael and what he wanted from her…and what she had to give him.

The terrible sadness rose in her. He deserved the best, someone who could be a full partner to him, who could give him children and a passionate love, not someone he'd have to take care of all their lives.

"Aaaiii."

The scream rent her thoughts to shreds. Pivoting toward the sound, she saw seven-year-old Maria Martinez leap off the front porch of her home and run down the driveway.

The child's dress was on fire!

"Maria, don't run," she shouted. "Roll on the grass. Drop and roll."

But panic ruled the child. She ran down the road, screaming in terror. Susan took off after her.

"Maria, here! This way! Come to me!"

The little girl cut across the lawn. Susan realized she was heading for the garden area, where her parents were probably gathering vegetables. Leaping a raised flower bed, she ran as fast as she could across the grass, desperate to stop the child.

Her breath came in great gasps as she exerted herself to the fullest. Halfway across the lawn, blackness gathered at the edges of her vision.

Please, God. Please let me save her. She's only seven. Please...let...her live....

Susan knew the moment her heart had given its all. Pain kicked in, harsh and overpowering. She pressed on, running, running, gaining on the figure in front of her that had become a dancing ball of fire in the center of her fading vision.

"Maria," she said, but could utter no more than a whisper now.

Blindly she ran toward the flames, guided by the shrieks of pain and terror as the blackness consumed her.

Faster, she ordered with each step.

Her body obeyed as it always had in the past. Power seemed to flow through her, the way it did when she danced Giselle, leaping and pivoting as if gravity had no claim on her being.

In front of her, the flames flickered like a playful nymph as she raced to catch them. Gathering all that she had left, she leaped, her arms reaching out blindly.

The flames seared her hands as she grabbed burning cloth. She hugged the small body of the child against her and fell to the ground, rolling...rolling...rolling until at last the darkness was complete, the shrieks faded into the drowning silence that filled her ears and there was nothing left but a deep void before her.

"Michael, I'm sorry," she whispered.

Then she fell into the great emptiness.

Eight

Michael was beat when he arrived at his condo in the wee hours of Monday morning. All he wanted was a quick shower and sleep. He'd been at the hospital for almost twenty-four hours, on his feet in surgery for sixteen of those, fighting for the life of a teenage boy who had suffered drug-induced heart failure.

The doorman took one look at his face, opened the elevator and punched in his floor. ''There you go, Doc.''

''Thanks,'' Michael mumbled, almost too tired to respond.

At the fourteenth floor, he heard the phone ringing before he unlocked the condo door. By the time he got inside, it had stopped. No one left a message.

Shrugging, he started stripping before he reached the shower. By the time he got there, he was ready to step in.

After washing up and turning the water off, he reached for a towel and realized the phone was ringing again. He got to the bedside in time to hear a hang-up. Why the hell didn't they leave a message?

Unaccountably irritated, he crawled into the sack and fell asleep almost before he pulled the sheet up to his armpits. The phone woke him up seven hours later.

"Hello?" he barked, not quite cordially.

"Hey, Doc," a man said.

Michael recognized the older man from the Mafia. "Oh, you." He yawned and glanced at the clock. Past noon. He should be at the office. However, he'd left word with his secretary and nurse that he wouldn't be in this afternoon as previously planned.

"Carmine has a deal for you."

Suppressing a sigh, Michael said, "Let's hear it."

"We can get a heart for your woman, too. There's one lined up for the boss, a man dying of cancer."

"That could be dangerous. Cancer cells can break off and spread to other parts of the body."

"Yeah, but this one is okay. So what do you say?"

"There's no way the hospital or I would agree to a black-market organ donation. It's too risky."

"Your woman needs one now. If you don't hurry, she might not need one at all."

The ominous tone irritated Michael. "What woman?"

"Susan Wainwright. According to the hospital report, she's stabilized and was airlifted out of Mission Creek about an hour ago."

"Airlifted to where?" Nothing made sense.

"Your hospital in Houston. Haven't you heard? She collapsed after saving some little girl who'd caught her clothes on fire. A real heroine."

Michael swung his legs off the bed and grabbed a pair of sweatpants tossed over a chair.

"We can probably have a heart there within an hour," the mobster offered.

"Get real," Michael said in a furious growl and hung up. He pulled a polo shirt over his head as he walked out of the bedroom. In the kitchen, he stepped into loafers, grabbed his wallet and headed down the elevator. He jogged the short distance to the hospital.

He found Susan in the cardiac wing, unconscious and on oxygen. "When did she get in?" he asked the nurse who was checking the IV.

"About fifteen minutes ago."

Michael read the brief notes on the emergency chart. She'd suffered mild burns on her hands and forearms, but nothing that wouldn't heal without a problem. The real trouble was internal. Quite simply, her heart had taken all it could.

Its beats had become so erratic, she couldn't get enough oxygen. The emergency team had handled that part, but it had been touch-and-go during the night. While he'd been in surgery or sleeping, her life had hung in the balance.

His review was interrupted by the senior ward

nurse, telling him of a meeting and that he was needed.

Grimly Michael went to the chief surgical resident's office. An emergency meeting convened shortly thereafter. Susan's name was moved to the top of the organ transplant list. "That is if she gave power of attorney over her health to a family member. If not, we'll have to wait until she's conscious and get her signature," the chief said.

Michael cursed silently. "I'll check on it. I'm sure some of her family are here."

"Most of them," the senior nurse reported. "In the third-floor waiting room."

Michael went to find them. Archy, Kate, Rose and Matt stood when he entered.

"Well?" Matt demanded.

Michael ignored his friend and glanced at Archy. "Do you have a power of attorney for her on health matters?"

Kate spoke up. "I do," she said. "Do you need me to sign something?"

"Yes, permission to operate when we get a donor heart for Susan."

"Will you do the surgery?" Matt asked.

Michael nodded. He met Matt's questioning glance levelly. "There will be four doctors on the team," he explained. "I'll supervise removing her heart while another team checks out the new one. If all is well, then I'll install the donor one."

Susan's father snorted in anger. "You make it sound like fixing the plumbing."

"Basically, that's what it is," Michael said calmly, familiar with a family's fears and frustrations.

The senior nurse stuck her head around the door. "You're needed, Dr. O'Day."

"Check at the cardiac desk," he told Kate. "The forms are there."

She nodded and followed after him.

"Uh, the patient is awake and asking for you," the nurse told him with an oblique glance at the mother.

"Susan is awake?" Kate asked.

The nurse nodded. "You'll have to scrub before you go in," she told Kate. "And put on a gown."

Several minutes later they entered Susan's room, both of them scrubbed and wearing surgical greens. The oxygen clip had been removed and her heartbeat was fairly steady, Michael noted, doing a quick sweep of the various machines hooked up to the patient.

He went to the bed and took her hand. Without thinking, he bent and kissed her, one quick brush of his lips over hers. Her mouth felt warm and soft. He crushed a need to gather her close. Her eyes were open when he lifted his head. "How are you feeling?" he asked.

"Fine." Susan smiled at the lie, then added, "Better."

"I've talked to the surgical board. You're at the top of the list for a donor heart."

"I wanted to talk to you about that." She saw her mother. "Mom, you're here."

"Most of us are. Justin will be here as soon as he can," Kate assured her daughter. "I was going to give permission for the operation." She looked anxiously from Susan to Michael. "Is it still up to me?"

"Not as long as Susan is coherent and can speak for herself. Will you sign the forms?" he asked the patient.

Susan looked from the quiet encouragement in his eyes to the worried look on her mother's face. "I think it's time," she said. "Yes, I'll sign."

"I'll get them," the nurse said, and hurried out.

"Can you tell me how Maria is? Is she...will she live?" Susan asked her mother.

Kate's smile was one of vast relief. "Maria is fine. She'll have a very short hairdo for a while and she'll sleep on her stomach, but her burns are mostly superficial except for a few spots on her upper back and neck."

"How did she catch on fire?" Susan asked.

"She was having a party for her doll and decided to light a candle the way her mother had for her birthday. She put it on the floor in front of the doll, then turned around and bent over to get her teapot out of the toy box. The back of her dress apparently was directly over the flame and caught fire. If you hadn't seen her in time—'' Kate pressed a hand over her lips and shook her head.

''She was running,'' Susan murmured. Odd, but it hurt to speak, as if she had strep throat. ''Flames were all up and down her back. I yelled and chased after her. Then things started going black and I was afraid I couldn't reach her.''

Michael lifted her hand to his lips. ''You saved her. The word is already out.''

She wanted to cling to him, but she refrained from reaching for him as an anchor of safety. She had to stand on her own two feet. ''How did you know I was here? Did the hospital call?''

''Somebody from Mission Creek called. It doesn't matter,'' he added when he saw the question forming on her lips. ''Ah, the forms.''

He took them from the nurse and showed her the places to sign. When it was done, the nurse witnessed the signature, then walked briskly from the room.

''How long?'' Susan asked.

''Before we get a heart?'' Michael shook his head. ''Only God knows that. You'll have to stay here until we do. Just in case—''

''In case my heart goes crazy again,'' she finished for him. ''It was terrible when I realized I might not reach Maria, that I couldn't catch her, a seven-year-old.''

''Don't think about it,'' Kate begged, patting her arm. ''Your father and Rose and Matt are here. Do you feel up to seeing them?''

Susan looked at Michael. He nodded. ''They can come in as soon as they scrub and put on surgical garb, provided they don't have colds or anything contagious. No one but immediate family will be allowed in. You might pass the word to her friends and the dance company.''

Kate left to tell the rest of the family. The room seemed too silent when she was alone with Michael. She watched him check the machine readouts, which showed her heart and breathing rates. ''What's that one?'' she asked, pointing to another number.

''The percentage of oxygen in your blood.''

''My, you can tell everything about a person these days, just by hooking one up to a machine.''

''Not everything.'' His smile flashed quick and brilliant. ''It doesn't read the female mind.''

''Are you really going to do the surgery?''

''Yes.''

She thought about it. ''I suppose making love once doesn't constitute a...personal involvement.''

He adjusted the IV drip into her arm. ''I think it does,'' he told her in no uncertain terms.

''I thought doctors couldn't operate on people they lo—they're involved with.''

His gaze speared into her. "I won't let anyone but the best touch you. You have my word on that. We have one of the most competent cardiac teams in the world at this hospital."

"But people die on operating tables, some from the trauma of the surgery if not the disease."

"That's a chance we have to take." He leaned over her. "I can divorce my feelings as a man from my skills as a surgeon. It's something a doctor has to learn early on. If he doesn't, he has a heart attack within ten years and is forced to do so or has to go into research, where he doesn't have to have direct contact with patients."

"I see."

Now that the surgery was a foregone conclusion, she found she was no longer worried about it or her future. In those moments of chasing after Maria, when her body began to fail her, she'd known she had no choice. It was either surgery or death. She could take her pick.

Sleep began to claim her. She wondered if he'd put something in the drip. "I'm not afraid," she said, her eyes refusing to stay open. "Not with you."

"I'll do the best I can" were the last words she heard before sinking down into blissfully peaceful darkness, which was not at all like the torturous moments when she ran blindly toward those dancing flames....

Michael half expected the two Mafia men to be at his condo when he arrived home late that evening. Fortunately the place was empty. He felt thankful for small favors.

He'd spent the afternoon in his office after all, seeing patients on referral, then had returned to the hospital to check on the teenager who had OD'd on drugs and to see how Susan was doing. She'd been quite cheerful.

An act, he decided, to reassure her family.

He'd met Susan's brother, Justin, sheriff of Lone Star County, who had flown in that afternoon. He had donated blood for her, as had her parents and Matt. Rose had been rejected due to her pregnancy. They would need twenty-seven pints of blood on standby before beginning the operation.

Michael rotated his shoulders, working out the tension. He debated going to the gym but decided it was too late. He was too tired and, besides, he wanted to be at home in case the hospital called. In case Susan needed him, he corrected with total honesty.

Before he had time to analyze the situation between them, the phone rang. He heaved an exasperated breath and picked it up.

"The offer still stands," a gravelly male voice said.

For a moment, he was tempted. He'd have to force the donor heart past the board, but to save Susan…

He sighed and rubbed a hand over his face. "It's generous, but tell Carmine no thanks."

The silence on the other end was ominous. The mobster finally found his voice. "I hope you don't live to regret this, Doc. If your woman dies, it'll be tough."

"She'll live, but thanks for your concern. Tell Carmine to come to my office next week for a thorough checkup. I'll see what we can do for him. Legally." Michael meant what he said. In spite of accusations of doctors playing God, he didn't judge his patients on their worth to society as a condition for surgery.

The man said he'd relay Michael's advice to the Mafia don and hung up.

Once in bed, Michael stared at the ceiling, his thoughts winging three blocks away to where Susan slept. His body stirred as he thought of her night here with him. He wanted more of those. Lots more.

A lifetime? Yeah.

Funny, a guy could go along not thinking of love or marriage or any of that stuff, positive he was immune to it, then *bang,* there it was, staring him right in the face.

But for the present he couldn't afford to think about the future. He had to concentrate on getting her through the surgery and the ordeal ahead.

He slept but a second it seemed, then the phone

started in again. He came instantly awake. "Yeah?" he said, expecting to hear the Mafia guy.

"Dr. O'Day?"

"Yes?"

"This is Kelly McNeil," one of the senior surgical nurses said. "We have a donor for Susan Wainwright."

"In town?" He glanced at the clock. Almost five. The sky glowed with the pink hues of dawn.

"Yes. An accident on I-10. The family has given consent."

"I'm on my way."

A life for a life, he mused a few minutes later, driving the three blocks to the hospital. At any other time, it would have been faster to walk. This morning he was in a hurry, and traffic was light.

The hospital board met in the conference room. Michael listened to the report from the attending physician, then looked over the chart of the victim. A girl, he saw, the same age as his niece. A life just beginning and already snuffed out.

Setting pity aside, he joined in the discussion of blood factors and an evaluation of the patients waiting for a heart. The decision was unequivocal. Susan was the closest match of the top ten on the list.

Before heading for surgery, he stopped by the waiting room where Archy and Kate, rumpled and tired, waited anxiously. They'd been awakened and informed of the possible surgery during the meeting. He assured them that things looked good for Susan.

Next he stopped by Susan's room. She was asleep from the drugs they'd started in her IV drip thirty minutes ago. He dropped a very light kiss on her lips, which were cool to his touch. Her face was pale. The oxygen tube was clipped to her nose again.

He checked her vital signs on the monitors. She was as ready as she would ever be. For a second he lingered, then he resolutely forced his thoughts to the task at hand.

An hour later Michael had his team assembled. He briefed them on the procedures and order of events. One thing he'd learned: There had to be someone in total control, coordinating each team's efforts so that they flowed smoothly, like two rivers coming together to form one. That would be him.

"Ready?" he asked.

The other three surgeons nodded. The four senior surgical nurses, already scrubbed, took their places, two in each operating room, which were side by side. Other nurses and technicians were already moving about. The other two doctors, the anesthesiologists, were at their stations.

Michael made one last check, then he nodded to each team. He took his place at the operating table. The door to his emotions closed and locked. The still form on the table was that of a patient needing all his concentration and skill in order to survive.

"Scalpel," he said.

Four hours later, he placed the last suture and stepped back from the table. It was done.

After Susan was safely in recovery and hooked up to the monitors, he removed his surgical garb and headed for the waiting room. There he found the Wainwright parents, siblings and Matt. They all stood.

"How is she?" Kate asked.

Michael smiled. "She came through just fine."

"When can we see her?"

"She'll be in recovery for the next eighteen hours."

"Eighteen hours," Justin repeated. "Isn't that long?"

"Not for this kind of surgery. However, you may scrub and go in, one at a time, for five minutes when she wakes up," he continued. "The nurse will come and get you." He looked at his watch. "It's nearly noon. Why don't we get some food? The cafeteria here is pretty good."

"Good idea," Archy said, taking Kate's arm. "Come on, Katie. We need something to protect our stomachs from the acid in the machine coffee."

Michael ate with the family, but said little except to answer their questions. After leaving them, he completed his office routine, worked out for an hour before going home, then returned to the hospital at nine that night.

Scrubbed and dressed in mask and gown, he stopped by the nurses' station before going to Susan's room. Her family had been in to see her and had gone to their hotel.

In her room, he looked over the monitors, touched her forehead, then pulled a chair close and took her hand.

Her skin was cool to the touch, her beautiful face as expressionless as a wax mask. He missed her fire and the sparks they struck off each other.

But that would come. Later. The next hours were crucial as her body and new heart began the long process of healing and adjustment. He yawned. It had been a long day.

Susan woke reluctantly. When she tried to move, she became aware of a hand holding hers. Rolling her head to the side, she saw dark hair against the white sheet.

"Michael?"

He stirred and raised his head. His smile was heartwarming. "Hi. How do you feel?"

"Like a big truck ran over my chest."

"Good. That's entirely normal."

"My throat is sore."

He nodded and brought a straw to her lips. "From the oxygen. It's so dry. Here, take a sip."

She took a drink of water, then realized it wasn't water. "Tastes like a sports drink."

"It's similar. You've passed the taste test, now let's see how you do at following directions. Squeeze my hand."

Watching his face, she did so. His expression

didn't change. She tried again, harder. "What are you looking for?"

"Reassurance," he said with a grin. "I wanted to see if you were strong enough for this."

Bending, he gave her a surprise kiss, very quick and light, but enough to warm her lips. "I've never been kissed through a mask before. It reminds me of Zorro."

The darkness began to close around her. She clung to his hand, which still held hers. Maybe, for now, that was okay. Tomorrow she would be stronger, she vowed. Then she wouldn't need him so much.

From deep within came a warning. It wasn't wise to depend on anyone too much. Love could come and go. Dancing had always been there for her.

"Go home," she whispered. "You need rest."

But he stayed until her senses shut down completely and she drifted in the endless sea of drugged sleep that erupted into pain each time she surfaced.

Michael frowned at Carmine Mercado. "You've been smoking. I told you to give it up."

"I'm sixty-four, too old for that nonsense."

"A man your age can expect to live to ninety," Michael informed him.

"Ah, who wants to live that long? I got no son. My nephew hasn't married and given us children for the future. What's to live for?"

"No more smoking," Michael said firmly, refusing to take up the don's lament.

Carmine smiled as innocently as a cherub. "Come on, Doc. It's one cigar a day. I don't even inhale."

"Smoking interferes with the body's ability to absorb oxygen. It puts an unnecessary strain on the heart. Either stop, or forget about surgery."

"What are my chances—slim to none?" Carmine shrugged aside his own mortality. "I know I'm far down the list. So how's the Wainwright girl?"

"The staff thinks she's a miracle. She's doing so well, we've moved her out of the ICU and into a room in the cardiac wing. Most patients spend three to five weeks in the hospital. She'll stay maybe two. If we can hold her in that long." His snort of laughter was wry.

"A fighter, huh? I like that. So how's my ticker?"

"The same as your doctor reported. You need to stay on your high blood pressure medication. You should have been on it years ago. Take an aspirin a day. If you take vitamins, check the amount of E. More than four hundred units a day and it acts as a blood thinner, too."

"Okay, okay. I'll be more careful."

Michael thought the chances of Carmine following orders were as likely as the chances of his getting a heart.

Oddly, after the week of tests—the same ones he'd administered to Susan the week before her collapse and consequent surgery—he'd developed a rapport with the old guy. Carmine Mercado was tough and dangerous, but there was also an aura of dignity about him and a sense of integrity—if one played by *his* rules.

Michael had made it clear he didn't play any kind of game with people's lives. Carmine had respected his stand and offered no more deals or veiled threats. He'd become simply another patient, one with a sense of humor about dying. He chuckled as he explained the jockeying going on behind the scenes to see who would succeed him.

"I'd like for my nephew, Ricky, to take over the business," he told Michael with the earnestness of a banker discussing the next CEO of his company. "But Frank…he's tough, not as smart as Ricky, but more ruthless."

The old man was really worried, Michael realized. It could only add to the stress on the overburdened heart, but he had no suggestions for his patient on this score.

"A man has to be firm to handle business, but I never did anything that wasn't necessary, you know?" Carmine continued thoughtfully. "I've never hurt women and children, either. A man's family ought to be sacrosanct."

"Mmm," Michael said. "Take a deep breath." He listened to the beating of the man's heart. Like Susan's before the operation, it was too fast, too hard and too erratic. "Okay, you can get dressed. I'll call you when I get the results of the final tests."

"Thanks, Doc. I appreciate your looking at me." This was said in a perfectly sincere tone, as if his goons hadn't visited or called Michael several times to add their not-so-subtle pressure in the decision.

Still following Spence's advice to string the don along, Michael had done the tests on the old guy and found he liked him. To a point.

"I'll do what I can," Michael said, "but I'm making no promises."

Carmine waved the disclaimer aside. "Okay, okay, I understand. Where am I on the list?"

"Second tier, actually. We don't have a numbered order since it depends on how well you match up to a donor. The patients in the highest group get first dibs, then those in the second group if there's no good match in the first."

"That's fair."

"I'm glad you think so," Michael said with a touch of rueful amusement. Had the don been less honorable, Michael supposed it wasn't beyond imagining his men disposing of those on the A list.

Since Mercado was his last patient, Michael left the office and headed for the hospital. There, he scrubbed, slipped into surgical garb and went in to see Susan.

"I feel as if I'm surrounded by bandits," she complained good-naturedly, eyeing his mask. "When do I get to go home?"

"When do you want to?"

She frowned suspiciously. "Tomorrow?"

"How about next Friday?"

"A week from today?"

"Yes."

Her green eyes widened in surprise. "Really?"

He laughed and chucked her under the chin. "Really. I'll fly you to the ranch. That will be a good place for you to convalesce."

"No way," she protested. "I feel great. I've talked to the ballet director. I can start back as assistant manager and chief fund-raiser as soon as I get a clean bill of health."

Michael shook his head. "No crowds for six months. That's an order," he added when she looked mutinous. "No shopping. No movies. No lunches at the country club."

"You've got to be kidding."

"If you do really well, maybe you can go to lunch after three months. You can't take a chance on infection," he told her seriously. "Your immune system is down."

She sighed. "I know. I take ninety pills a day to keep it that way."

He couldn't resist when she pursed her delectable lips. He bent toward her. He had to touch her, even if it was through a gauze mask.

Emotion flickered in her eyes, then she looked away and lowered her head. He stopped and studied her.

"I really think I'll be able to do normal things soon. I can already tell a difference in how I feel. The shortness of breath and the chest pain are gone. Maybe I'll start looking for my dream man."

Although her tone was teasing, something hot and furious flashed through Michael. With rigid control, he suppressed it. He knew about the dangers inherent in a doctor-patient relationship, the dependency syndrome and all that. It worked both ways. Doctors, in caring for someone through a dangerous situation, could also fall for their patients.

"I'm really grateful for all you've done," she continued, her eyes and smile filled with such total trust it squeezed his insides like a vise.

Patients had been known to think they were in love with their doctors when what they felt was gratitude. Had she realized that was what she felt?

With her streak of independence and stubborn nature, he'd trusted his instincts on this one. Had he been wrong?

"I merely did my job," he told her, ignoring the questions that speared through him. After checking her chart, he went to the gym and worked until he was exhausted enough to sleep.

His dreams were restless, though, all mixed up with the Mafia trying to steal Susan's heart while he tried desperately to get her to a safe place.

Nine

"I'm excited," Susan admitted, peering out the window of Michael's car, a dark-blue sedan he kept in Houston. "Everything looks so new and different."

"One's view of the world does change after a close-call experience," he agreed.

She stole a glance at him. During her days in the hospital, there had been times when he'd looked at her with passion in his eyes, but mostly he'd been very professional in his manner.

That was just as well. She'd decided a doctor-patient relationship was all they shared. The night of passion had been a mistake, a weakness on her part. And his.

Her family thought he walked on water. He'd been kind and unfailingly polite to them, answering all their questions patiently and completely. He'd been the same with her. Reassuring. Encouraging. Wonderful.

The perfect physician.

Her watch pulsed against her wrist. "Pill time," she muttered, reaching for the pill container and wa-

ter bottle in her purse. "I'm really tired of pills."
She swallowed them down.

His smile was sympathetic, albeit somewhat distant. He seemed focused on other things this morning.

Pressing a hand to her chest, she realized the ache
there was from a different cause than it had been two
weeks ago when she'd been taken to the hospital in
Mission Creek, then transferred to Houston.

After the surgery, with hours and hours of nothing
to do but contemplate the future, she'd done research
on the Net, using her laptop. Her chances of leading
a normal life, as in having a home and raising a
family, were slender.

Getting through the next five years would be a
miracle, it appeared. With the multiple pill-taking
and a constant wariness of infection, she would be a
burden to anyone who shared her life. So she'd come
to a decision.

If she was going to be a semi-invalid the rest of
her life, however long *that* was, she wouldn't impose
her frailties on anyone else, especially the man beside her, who had already gotten her through surgery
and gently talked her through the days of pain and
nights of doubt that followed.

Never, she vowed, would she cling to Michael's
strength like a leech. He was a wonderful person and
he deserved more from his mate.

If she ever married, it wouldn't be out of need and

fear, but as an equal. That was her decision. Now she had to put it into action.

"Home," he said, interrupting the restless workings of her mind.

Home was her mother's condo. She wasn't allowed to be alone for a second. If all went well for the next two weeks, she could perhaps return to her one-bedroom apartment.

She longed for solitude and the relief of not having to constantly guard her feelings so her family wouldn't worry.

"The grass looks so incredibly green after yesterday's rain," she murmured, concentrating on the cool expanse of lawn and lovely flower beds at the condos lining a man-made lake on the outskirts of Houston.

"The temperature has cooled, too. October is a great month for convalescing, warm enough for outdoor walks, cool enough to be comfortable," he said, parking and turning off the engine.

She thought of walks with him, of dinner on a terrace overlooking downtown and of nights filled with delight.

The idea sent her new heart into overdrive, but now it wasn't alarming. It merely felt normal. She wondered how long it would be before she was a whole human being again, how long before she could make love.

"Other than staying away from crowds and getting plenty of rest, are there, uh, any other restrictions on my activities?'' she asked, then wondered if he could read her thoughts when he flicked a perceptive glance her way.

''Not really. You can do anything you feel up to.''

She felt his withdrawal as a tangible thing. Since the surgery, he'd become very circumspect, other than a few light touches of his lips, usually through a mask.

''And if I feel like going to your place?'' she said with a flirty coyness she detested in other women. She realized it was a defensive ploy. By treating the situation lightly, as a flirtation, she could pretend the answer didn't matter.

''I think your mother is expecting you.''

Which didn't tell her a thing. Maybe he didn't see her as a woman now that he'd performed the surgery. She was just another patient. Remembering her vow not to be a burden on anyone, she reaffirmed that resolve.

''True.'' She hooked a tendril of hair behind her ear. ''I need a haircut. Okay if I go to the beauty salon if it's after hours, with only the stylist there?''

''Let's see how you do first,'' he suggested. ''Two more weeks without complications, then you can have more freedom to come and go, up to a point.''

He carried her small piece of luggage and a plastic bag filled with a washbasin, soap, powder, lotion and a box of tissues from the hospital, which the nurse had insisted she take home.

"Susan! Michael!" her mother exclaimed, opening the door before they rang the bell, her manner cheerful, her eyes anxious. "Come in. Are you hungry? Or do you need to rest first? I made a pan of brownies with pecans."

Susan managed a smile. "I'm not tired at all. Brownies would be great."

"Put the luggage there," Kate told Michael, indicating the foyer floor. "Let's go out to the terrace. Is that okay? Can Susan go outside?"

"It's fine. In fact, she should walk every day, weather permitting," Michael explained. "Let her be the judge of what she feels like doing, as long as she doesn't overdo. Remind her to wear a mask outside."

"Of course. Would you like a cup of coffee?" Kate asked. "Or tea?"

"I'd prefer iced tea," Michael replied.

"Same here." Knowing her mother needed to feel useful, Susan let herself be led to a chair and pampered with her favorite foods. The need to be alone increased. When her mother left the room, she wished Michael would go, too.

As if sensing her thoughts, Michael took a chair beside her and said, "Depression is normal after major surgery. You'll want to withdraw from everyone.

The syndrome feeds upon itself, so try not to give in to it.''

"Don't you have a pill for that?'' She didn't hide the sting of sarcasm.

He grinned. "Yes. You're getting a mild one in your daily mix. But you'll still be a grouch.''

She managed a laugh. "I won't throw any more barbs at you if you won't throw any more at me.''

"I only tell the truth. Ah, Kate. I was just telling your daughter that she'll be hard to live with for a while. It's normal, but watch out for her sharp tongue.''

Kate glanced at him, then Susan. "I'll wear armor.'' She served the tea and a plate of brownies.

Susan had a feeling her mother knew of the attraction that had existed between her and the handsome surgeon and was delighted at the idea. It would be convenient to have a doctor in the family, she decided on a cynical note, in case she collapsed again.

Shaking her head slightly, she wondered why she felt so negative. The doldrums, as Michael had warned?

She admitted the possibility. It seemed she'd had to give up everything—her career, any thoughts of a future, the passion they had shared—and for what? A heart that her body might or might not accept.

Involvement with anyone was out of the question

until she was certain she could stand on her own and not be a spineless, clinging vine. When would that time come?

On Friday of the second week after going to stay with her mother, Susan looked expectantly at Michael in the exam room of his Houston offices. Lightly tanned from her daily walks, she felt truly rested for the first time in months. She could now stroll an hour at a time, not as fast as she once would have, but still, she was making progress. Her family was delighted.

"You're a miracle," he said, flashing a smile her way when he looked up from the test results. "You did great on the stress test. The liver enzymes are good. There're no signs of rejection."

"Can I stop taking the pills?" she asked.

"No, but you can cut back to eighty a day."

She groaned in exasperation, then perked up. "Since I'm doing so well, I think I'll go to the ballet tonight. It's a benefit for the new children's wing of the hospital."

"No crowds," he told her sharply.

"I'll be in a box by myself. The director arranged it. I'll slip in after the house lights are dimmed. No one will know I'm there."

"Who will be with you?"

"No one."

He gave her an irritated frown and shook his head.

"You can't be running all over town by yourself. How will you get to the theater?"

"Taxi."

He frowned at her in open exasperation. "No. You don't know who has been in them or what kind of germs are in those cars. Where's your mother?"

"She left for Mission Creek after lunch today to visit with Gran at the nursing home."

"What time shall I pick you up?"

Her hackles rose at his tone. "I don't need anyone to baby-sit me. I'll arrange for a limo."

"That's no better than a cab. I'll be by at seven. The ballet usually starts at eight, doesn't it?" He narrowed his eyes in a menacing fashion. "How the hell did you get here?"

"It really isn't your concern."

He cursed under his breath. "You came in a taxi," he concluded. "I'll be finished here in another thirty minutes. Wait in my office. I'll take you home, then to the ballet."

She argued, but the doctor had made up his mind. She was ushered into his office, the door firmly closed after her. She stood by the window and looked at the small park where mothers watched their children and chatted.

One toddler kept heading out on his own toward the street. His mother finally set him firmly in the sandbox and stood guard to make sure he stayed.

A heaviness settled on her spirits as she watched.

Home and hearth seemed much more important to her now. Her family had been wonderfully thoughtful during her recovery, sending her gifts to cheer her—funny e-mails, baskets of flowers, books, videos, anything to ease the boredom of her days.

Not that she'd felt like doing a lot. After having her breastbone cracked down the middle and propped open, she'd expected to be sore, but being run over by a truck didn't begin to describe the initial pain. The daily walks had been a struggle of mind over body the first week.

Today was Friday. Monday would mark four weeks since her collapse from chasing after Maria. At times during the past month, she'd found it very hard to fight the dark feelings that would roll over her suddenly and for no good reason. Underlying those was sadness, a knowledge that her fate would never be hers to command as it once had.

She felt an intense longing that had nothing to do with her health and everything to do with her heart—with the emotional part of it and with the part of herself that wanted desperately to feel like a woman again.

Hearing Michael's deep voice in the hall outside the door caused that organ to beat fiercely. He was the center of that longing.

Closing her eyes tightly, she refused to give in to either the longing or the darkness. She would get past this on her own. She would. She must.

The office door opened. "Ready?" he asked.

A smile was almost more than she could manage, but she did. Picking up her purse, she followed him down a corridor and into a private elevator at the back of the building.

"Luckily, I drove this morning since I had an early call from the hospital," he said, taking her arm and leading the way to the blue sedan in a numbered parking space.

"You work too hard," she began, then stopped. His working hours were not her business.

"It's been busy of late," he admitted. "I haven't taken Friday afternoon off in a month or so."

Because of her and others like her who needed him to make them well, she acknowledged. But she was well now. She could take care of herself.

He drove straight to her mother's condo and whisked her inside. The mantel clock chimed six when they entered. The sound echoed through the empty rooms. Susan suddenly missed her mother's cheerful chatter.

After putting her purse on the foyer table, she lingered with her back to him. "I've changed my mind about the ballet. It's probably better that I don't go."

He removed his suit jacket and tie, then tossed both on a chair back. "No, it'll be good for you. You're too active to play the invalid for long. I should have realized that. Let's order in. Chinese, pizza, deli?"

"Deli. Corned beef on rye with sauerkraut and hot mustard. Other than an occasional brownie, Mother has kept me on mashed bananas and mush in the belief that regular food would be too much of a strain on my heart."

He chuckled at her wry remark. "Deli it is. I'll call. I know a great place that delivers."

When she offered him a glass of wine, he accepted, then suggested she join him on the patio. They left the door open in order to hear the doorbell.

Susan sighed as she took a seat. Michael stretched his long legs straight out, the wineglass propped on his flat abdomen as he settled next to her and observed the land around them. She used the time to study him.

He was as handsome as ever with his dark hair and eyes as blue as a summer day. When he lifted the glass, she stared at his hands and the long fingers that could perform the most intricate surgery…or the most delicate of caresses.

Magic. Delight. Breathless passion.

She'd known all those with him. She wanted them again. Trembling as new waves of longing rushed over her, she held tight to her resolution to need no one.

Invalid. While she didn't feel like one, she knew she would forever be tied to pills and tests. She knew she would never perform onstage again.

Without her mother knowing, she'd tried some

very gentle stretching exercises, then a few pliés and jetés yesterday. After fifteen minutes, she'd been trembling from head to foot from the effort. She thought it would be a long, long time before she could dance, run, make love...

"If you keep looking at me like that, I'll be forced to kiss you," Michael announced in a casual manner.

His statement startled her. She tore her gaze from his. "Germs," she reminded him, feeling shaky with longing.

"I scrubbed before leaving the office. I don't have a cold. You're doing well. It should be safe enough."

Before she could frame a reply, he had acted on the thought. With easy strength, he lifted her into his arms and placed her in his lap. Then his mouth sought hers.

For about a tenth of a second, she thought of refusing. The ridiculous idea dissolved in a frothy mist of delight as his lips closed over hers. Crystal shards of joy spiraled outward from that point of contact to every part of her.

"I've wanted to do that for days, weeks," he murmured against her mouth.

"You stayed away," she reminded him. "You rarely came over, not even when my mother called and invited you to dinner." She'd hated herself for listening for his step and the ringing of the doorbell announcing his presence, for the yearning that choked her when she thought of him.

"You needed the time to recover without complications. I don't think I could have resisted you otherwise."

"But you don't have to now?"

"No. I'm not your doctor anymore. Now we're a man and a woman with only this between us."

He kissed her again. One hand cupped her shoulder while the other made magic along her back, leaving a trail of sparkles down her spine, up her side and finally over on her breast. The tip beaded as he caressed lightly.

She wondered how far he intended to go. And if she should let him.

Before she could find an answer in the whirling mist, the doorbell rang. With a deeply inhaled breath, he gently placed her in the chair, then went to answer. In a few minutes, he was back, carrying two covered containers that emitted a spicy aroma. She realized she was hungry for food as well as caresses. And that she was going to have to be the one to break off this senseless passion between them.

Michael observed Susan closely during the ballet performance. The show was long, and by the end, her graceful body had slumped into the velvet chair. She sighed wearily as they applauded the final act.

"Let's go." He wanted to get her out while the

cast was taking their bows, before anyone spotted the former prima ballerina and rushed to the theater box.

Leading her down the dim stairs and out the stage door, he had a running argument about his intentions. He should return her to her mother's home and hit the road. That was what he should do. He wasn't sure he could.

Not that he was going to make love to her. She was too exhausted for passion, although it sometimes simmered between them when their eyes met. But he wanted to stay with her, to hold her while she slept.

He smiled at the image. He'd never considered himself an altruistic person, but since meeting this woman, something in him had changed. Falling in love had its interesting quirks.

Once in the condo, he urged her to sit. "The show was long. You're worn out."

"I think I'd like to change."

"Good idea. Put on your pajamas. I'll make us a cup of hot chocolate."

She turned on him in fury, surprising him. "I don't need your nurturing. I get that from my mother."

"What do you want?" he demanded, hunger growing as he thought of the possibilities.

"To be treated like a woman, not an invalid who can't get across the street by herself. You, my mother, my whole family, in fact, act as if I'll collapse at any moment.''

She stopped abruptly, as if giving away too much. He thought he understood what the problem was. ''I think of you as a woman,'' he assured her. ''Do you think you're any less desirable now than before the surgery?''

Shrugging, she laid the green silk shawl that matched her dress on the sofa arm.

''I want to make love to you, but you're not ready.''

''You're right.'' Meeting his gaze levelly, she added, ''I think it would be better not to see each other.''

''What?'' He wasn't sure what he'd expected to hear, but it hadn't been this. ''Why?''

''I think part of my...attraction to you was born of need. I didn't want to admit it, but I knew I had no choice about the heart replacement. You were the best and I needed your expertise. I've been clinging to you, but now, I think I should stand on my own two feet. It would be easier without the complication of sex.''

Michael subdued the fury and the urge to sweep her into his arms and show her just how much she still needed him in ways that had nothing to do with his skill as a surgeon.

''I see,'' he murmured. ''I agree. I've been aware of the doctor-patient dependency factor from the moment I knew of your condition. It was a complication between us, but I don't consider it one now. There's also the passion. It hasn't gone away.''

He watched as she took a deep breath and exhaled slowly. He sensed a fragility about her that hadn't previously been there, or else she'd kept it hidden behind her stubborn will.

Which was the real Susan Wainwright?

''True.'' She met his eyes with her usual candor. ''But I don't want to give in to it. I have to find a new direction for my life. I think I could do that better without passion.''

''Without me?''

''Yes. I'm sorry—''

He waved the apology aside. ''Don't be. I've admired your grit and honesty from the moment we met.''

''I'm grateful—''

''That,'' he said in a harsher voice, ''is the one thing I don't want from you.''

She nodded.

He hesitated, torn between a desire to remind her of the feelings between them, as well as the passion, and a sense of honor that demanded he leave as she requested.

''Stay away from crowds. Don't forget to take your pills. Walk every day. Rest often,'' he ordered, and heard the irony in his words. He turned and left before he made a fool of himself.

On the road to his place, he reflected on the ironies of fate and the fact that he'd forgotten his own golden rule: Never get emotionally involved with a patient. He'd known the lovely ballerina was a heartbreaker that very first day he saw her in Mission Ridge.

He parked in the underground garage and grimly jogged up the fourteen sets of stairs to the penthouse, but found he was still too restless for sleep.

Okay, I've made a mistake, he admitted.

So get over it.

That might be easier said than done. He closed his eyes and tried counting sheep.

Ten

"**Y**ou're full? I see. Thanks anyway," Susan said to the woman at the airline shuttle service. After hanging up, she hesitated for a full five minutes before calling Michael.

His voice was groggy when he answered.

"Uh, this is Susan. I was wondering if you were flying to Mission Ridge today?" At the silence on the end of the line, she quickly added, "Mom called. My grandmother is ill. The shuttle is full, so I wondered if you were going."

She wished she hadn't called.

"I'll pick you up in half an hour," he said, now fully alert and cheerful.

Sounding stiff and artificial, she murmured, "Thank you," then hung up as if the phone were too hot to handle.

She flew around the condo, getting her stuff together, determined to return to her own place after she made sure Gran was okay. When the doorbell rang, she was ready.

Or she thought she was until she saw Michael standing there, dressed in a white polo shirt, navy cargo shorts and jogging shoes, sunglasses perched on top of his head. Her heart did a dip, a spin and a leap, then settled to beating frantically as she tried to think of a clever greeting.

"Hi," she finally said.

A muscle twitched in his jaw. Rather than speaking, he simply nodded and grabbed her suitcase and the plastic bag still packed with the stuff left from the hospital stay.

"Would you mind stopping by my place? I want to leave most of this and check my mail."

"No problem."

She locked the door behind them and followed him to his car. After he asked, she directed him to her apartment, having forgotten that he'd never been there. Odd, but their lives were enmeshed on so many different levels that it seemed as if he should know everything about her.

Pressing a hand to her chest, she admitted he did know nearly everything. But not all. He didn't know that she woke during the night, restless and unhappy, filled with longing to be in his arms.

No. She wouldn't allow herself to think of that.

"What's wrong? Are you having chest pains?"

Blinking at him, she shook her head and lowered her hand. "I was just…thinking."

"You said your grandmother was nearly ninety?" he asked, sympathy in his voice.

Susan nodded. "It would be hard to give her up,"

she began, then stopped. His parents had died when he was young. She'd had Gran for twenty-seven years.

He parked and turned to her. "I'll carry your things." He ducked his head and peered into her eyes. "Are you crying?" he asked gently.

Before she could deny it, his arms were around her, drawing her close, surrounding her in warmth and safety.

"I'm fine. Let me go," she demanded.

His face changed in an instant, becoming as opaque as stone. "Sorry." He released her.

She rushed up the sidewalk and into the place she'd lived for six years. It felt like a foreign land, strange and barren, when she opened the door. Behind her, Michael stopped at the threshold, set her luggage inside and returned to his car.

After checking the mail and phone messages, she pushed the bags out of the way and closed the door, then turned the dead bolt. For the tenth time, she wished she hadn't called him. She could have chartered a flight.

Getting in the sedate dark sedan, she compared it with the flashy sports car he kept in Mission Ridge. Michael himself was a complicated personality, she thought as she looked at him. She'd seen him as a friend, as a doctor and as a lover. He was bold, confident, maybe arrogant, but he was also kind and nurturing. Most of all, he was exciting, passionate and giving.

"Stop it. Unless you mean it," he muttered in a low growl, braking at a red light.

"What?" As soon as she asked, she knew what he meant. He'd caught her staring. Heat slid into her face. "Sorry."

He heaved a breath, then took off when the light changed. At the airport, he ran through the preflight check with the total concentration she'd learned to expect of him. In a few minutes, they were airborne.

The hour-long trip was accomplished in near silence. After he landed and secured the plane in his hangar, he motioned toward the house. "Give me a minute to check my answering machine, then I'll take you home."

"To my grandmother's place, please. She lives in Sunny Acres. It's closer than the ranch. My mom will be there."

He nodded and went inside.

She waited on the patio, aware of the peace and beauty surrounding his home. She thought of children playing on the lawn, a dog running at their heels. He would make a wonderful father. And husband. Some woman would be lucky.

Hot tears sprang into her eyes. She wanted to be that woman, his wife, the mother of his children. There were feelings between them, as well as passion. Why not take everything life offered?

Desperation seized her. She wanted to, so very much. She had only to reach for him and bind him to her through passion and his innate compassion.

She couldn't. To go to him now would be unfair, a sign of weakness on her part. She had to prove herself first and show him and her family that she could make it on her own, that she wasn't an invalid who needed constant attention.

"Ready," he said, returning and leading the way inside the neat garage, which housed only the car.

In the sporty convertible, with the October breeze blowing her hair, the longing receded. The day was beautiful beyond description, making her spirits suddenly buoyant. "On days like this, it's difficult not to feel invincible, to feel as if the world was here just for our pleasure."

Clamping down on her bottom lip, she wished she hadn't mentioned pleasure. It conjured up images she didn't want to invoke between them.

"Maybe it is. All animals were created with an inborn sense of pleasure, a gift, as it were."

She watched his strong hands on the wheel as he pulled under the portico at the nursing home. They were capable of pleasure and comfort and saving lives. He deserved a mate who could match his strengths. A nurse perhaps, one of those who stood by him at the operating table—

"Here we are," he reminded gently, a smile tilting the corners of his mouth.

"Oh. Yes. Well, thank you for the lift."

He nodded, reached across her and opened the door. For the briefest instant, his arm crossed her midsection, leaving a burning path of yearning there. She got out and waved as he closed the door. He gave her a half salute and drove off. From inside the glass doors to the senior care facility, she watched him leave. Her heart went with him.

"Susan," her mother said in surprise. "I thought that was Michael when I saw the car. I'm delighted you're here."

"I thought I would see about Gran, then spend a few days at the ranch. How is she?"

Kate frowned and shook her head. "She has pneumonia. So you can't go in. I'll tell her you stopped by."

Susan burst into tears.

"There, dear, there now. Don't cry. Gran will be all right. She's quite strong, a fighter, the doctor said, just as Michael said you were."

Susan sobbed harder, not at all sure why she was crying or why she felt so desperately sad.

The phone was ringing when Michael walked into his house. Sitting on a stool at the island counter, he grabbed the receiver. "O'Day here."

"Hey, Doc," a gruff voice said.

"How's Carmine?" Michael asked, recognizing the old man's henchman.

"Not so good. He's asking for you."

This news gave Michael pause. "Where is he?"

"At home."

"Give me the address." He wrote it down, changed to slacks and a white shirt, then drove down the curving road, off the ridge where he lived, to Goldenrod, a community on the road to Mission Creek.

"This way," the older mobster said, letting him in the impressive mansion. He ignored Frank Del Brio and others who were gathered in the living room.

Michael noticed the absence of conversation. He recognized Carmine's brother, Johnny, and his nephew, Ricky. Both men looked tired. Three other men were present, but no women.

It occurred to Michael that, other than his bodyguards and presumably some servants, the old don lived in this huge house alone. When he entered the bedroom, he was taken aback at Carmine's appearance. The Mafia boss seemed to have shrunk in the three weeks since he'd seen him. His face was pasty, his crafty gaze dim with pain. An oxygen tank stood beside the massive four-poster bed.

"Carmine," he said, going to the bedside and shaking the cold, waxy-feeling hand. Michael recognized the signs of a rapidly failing heart.

"Good of you to come," Carmine rasped. "I

wanted to tell you…I'm going to leave you the half mil.''

''I won't take it.''

''Give it to the hospital then, whatever you want.''

Michael shook his head. ''Leave it directly to the hospital, if that pleases you, but count me out.''

''Stubborn pup,'' the old man muttered, anger brightening his gaze for a moment.

Michael shrugged.

''If I'd had a son, he'd 'a been like you. When I was in my heyday, I could whip my weight in bobcats, thought I owned the world and nothing could touch me. Like you.''

Hiding his pity, Michael grinned. ''Tough, huh?''

''Forget the Wainwright girl. That family is too proud. Get you a good woman. My wife was a fine one. She died twenty years ago…missed her every single day.''

Looking into the old man's eyes, Michael thought this was true. A man on his deathbed tended to count his blessings, once he stopped ranting against his fate. Most of them tried to make up for past sins. Carmine was at that point.

The old man paused for a moment, fighting for breath. Michael checked the oxygen flow on the tank, then clipped the tube to Carmine's pajama top when he shook his head, indicating he didn't want it on his nose. The scent of a cigar clung to the old man.

"No smoking," Michael reminded him.

"You doctors, always fussing."

The two men grinned at each other.

Carmine sucked in several breaths, then spoke again. "I already left the hospital a half million in your name. The other half mil is in cash, there on the table."

Startled, Michael glanced at a leather briefcase on a low table in front of a sofa with gold leaf on its scrolled back and legs. "Better put it in a safe. It might disappear when you're gone."

The old man laughed, then coughed several times before speaking again. "It will. What's it to me now?"

Michael had an idea. "Tell your men to give it to the children's wing of the local hospital, an endowment for the children you should've had. I think you'd have been one hell of a father."

"Good or bad?" the old man joked.

"Good," Michael said sincerely.

Carmine waved this aside. "Take care," he murmured, his eyes drooping as weariness overtook him. "You're a good man. I wish..."

Michael waited, but the don said nothing more. A hand touched his elbow, and he looked quickly around at the older mobster, who had tears in his eyes. They went into the hall.

"You heard about the money?" Michael asked.

The man nodded. "It'll be taken care of."

Michael knew Carmine's last wishes would be carried out. In his car, the sun on his face and the wind in his hair, he felt the weight of mortality on his shoulders. The brevity of life seemed much more real.

He wanted a good woman at his side, but she didn't seem to want him, not since the surgery. There were still sparks between them, but he wouldn't lure her with passion. She had to come to him freely because she wanted a future with him, not because of overwhelming desire.

Not that the passion hadn't been great.

Susan was strong willed. Dancing was her first love, her true passion. If she could find some way to express that, either through teaching or dancing again, she evidently didn't need anything else.

That was what he'd thought about his own life...until he'd met her.

Kate Wainwright felt like a sneak in her own home—actually, the one-bedroom cottage Archy insisted she use—as she lifted the phone and dialed a number. On the third ring, she decided to hang up, but then Michael answered.

"Hello," she said. "This is Susan's mother."

"Hello, Kate. What can I do for you?"

His manner was so relaxed and easy, she immediately felt better about calling him first thing on a Sunday morning. "Well, it's Susan," she said.

"Is she okay? I hope she hasn't fallen off a horse again."

"No, no, it's nothing like that. She burst into tears yesterday at the nursing home when I told her she couldn't see Gran because of pneumonia. Susan never cries."

The long pause at the other end alarmed her, but finally he spoke.

"Depression is normal after any kind of surgery, especially a major operation as Susan had. All the body's resources are tied up in healing."

"But she's been so cheerful all month. She did everything she was supposed to. She walked—and wore the mask while she did—and ate everything on her plate and went to bed early." She paused to think about this odd behavior. "That isn't like Susan, is it?"

"She's usually a rebel," he agreed, "but she wants to get well as fast as she can. That's probably why she's being so good."

Kate sighed. "I don't know. Something's bothering her, but when I asked, she went back to being Pollyanna. I must admit it worries me."

"I'll be around this week. I'll check on her."

"That would be great," Kate admitted, relieved to put her daughter in his capable hands. "I wondered if you would be available to come to dinner tonight? Susan and Justin are going to join me. I need to speak to them about the provisions in Gran's will, as she requested.''

''Won't I be in the way?''

''No, I'll speak to them before you arrive. Come around seven. Is that too early?''

''No, that's fine. I'll see you then.''

Kate hung up. She realized her hand was trembling. It was seldom that she interfered in her children's lives, but she sensed a darkness in Susan that frightened her. She hoped she'd done the right thing.

Sighing, she acknowledged it was difficult to tell with these modern young people. She wanted happiness for her youngest child above all else. Susan was in love with Michael, whether she admitted it or not. Kate wanted them to have a chance.

She thought of her own life. Perhaps if she'd been more willing to listen to Archy years ago, they might have been together today, but she'd been so hurt upon finding he'd had an affair and fathered a child with a Native American woman.

She'd never suspected, but then, she'd been so involved with their children. She'd had their son, then the girls had come along.

Life had been so rushed and busy with them and the charity projects she'd sponsored. There'd been no time to give to her marriage. Like the sun that faithfully came up each morning, she'd thought Archy would always be there.

* * *

Michael dressed, then drank a glass of orange juice as a bid to vitamins and good health while waiting for the toaster to pop up a couple of waffles.

He tried not to think of Susan while he ate, or later, while he loaded his golf clubs into the convertible and drove to the country club. On a success scale of one to ten, he'd give himself about a one.

At the club, he found Flynt and Tyler waiting. With them was Cara Carson, Flynt's sister and twin to Fiona, the other Carson daughter. Cara was an English teacher at the local high school, a quiet sort of person, unlike Fiona, who spent her days in pursuit of fun.

Cara was shorter than Susan and had dark hair, green eyes and a beauty mark above her lip on the left side. Her twin had the same beauty mark, but on the right side, making them mirror images of each other.

Referring to his rotation through pediatrics, Michael recalled that the timing of the split was critical in the development of identical twins. Around ten hours after conception, the split produced regular identical twins; between ten and thirteen hours, the twins were mirror images; after thirteen hours, the split was usually incomplete and the twins were joined.

"Cara is taking Spence's place this morning," Flynt told him. "He's tied up with something."

"Glad to have you along, Cara," Michael said sincerely. He asked about her classes this year.

"I have two honors and two regular classes, plus some tutoring of special students. It's a nice mix. No troublemakers this year."

Her smile was bright and her eyes sparkled. She was an excellent golfer, not spectacular but with a steady swing that hit the ball straight and true. He wondered why he couldn't have fallen for someone like her.

With an inward sardonic laugh, he reminded himself that an entanglement with another green-eyed vixen hadn't been in his plans for the foreseeable future, either, not until he nearly ran over the tall, willowy beauty who moved with the grace of a reed blowing in the wind.

"Did Spence say anything about the Bridges case?" Flynt asked Tyler.

"No, but Carmine Mercado died during the night. I wonder if Spence is checking records before Carmine's bank accounts are tied up in probate."

"He won't find anything in them," Michael said, thinking of the half million sitting in a briefcase near the dying man's bed. "The old man was too crafty for that."

"What does the Mafia do?" Cara asked as they walked up to the next tee.

Tyler lined up his shot. "Launders money, I understand. Brings in goods from Mexico and sells them without benefit of license, which makes it easier to forget to pay taxes on them, too. Supplies the illegal labor market.'' He hit a straight shot down the fairway.

Michael thought of the Texas mob and wondered why, if everyone knew of their activities, the FBI couldn't catch them and put a stop to it. Maybe their hands were tied unless someone complained or offered information or helped them gather evidence. Maybe they needed an insider who could report on the illegal activities of the gang.

''I understand Frank Del Brio has already made his move to take over,'' Tyler added as he stepped aside and Cara placed her ball on the tee.

''I wonder what Ricky thinks of that,'' Flynt said, hitting after his sister.

''He won't like it,'' Cara answered. ''He always wanted to be the leader when you guys ran around together. But Luke was the real boss.''

''Hey, your big brother didn't take orders from anyone,'' Flynt protested.

Cara grinned. ''Okay, but Luke was the instigator of most of the episodes that got you boys into trouble.''

Tyler chuckled. ''He's probably on some tropical island, causing trouble with a dozen female hearts, as we speak.''

Michael wished he could cause some serious trouble to one female heart. She'd certainly wreaked havoc with his. Thinking of dinner that night, he wondered if he should head back to Houston and stay there.

Susan glanced at the three settings her mother was placing on the table. ''I thought you said Justin wouldn't be here.''

''He won't. He's working on a case.'' Kate paused, worry in her eyes. ''I wonder if it's something to do with the Mafia. Carmine Mercado died during the night.''

''Unless Justin caught them red-handed rustling cattle or something, he wouldn't be investigating them. That's the FBI's job. Is Dad coming over?''

Kate shook her head.

At that moment, Susan heard a vehicle in the driveway. Looking out, she spied Michael's sports car. ''Oh.''

''Is that Michael? I asked him over to thank him for bringing you home yesterday.''

''Mother, are you trying a little matchmaking?''

The older woman looked flustered for a second, then lifted her chin haughtily. ''I learned long ago not to interfere in my children's love lives.''

''Good.'' Susan marched to the door. ''I'll let him in.''

She opened the cottage door and waited for the handsome surgeon. He wore dark slacks and a white shirt, the cuffs rolled back to reveal tanned arms. For a second she wanted to rush down the sidewalk and into those arms.

"Good evening," she called with false cheer. "How was the golf game?"

He frowned, then grinned. "I came in dead last. Flynt bragged all during lunch. I considered choking him, but there were too many people around, including his sister."

"Fiona was with you?" Susan ignored the painful stab that went through her chest. Fiona Carson was a flighty, silly female without a serious thought in her head. She was also very attractive.

"No, Cara. She's a good player and a good sport."

"High praise, indeed," Susan murmured, her hackles rising even as she smiled. The weight that had taken up residence on her spirits shifted and settled even more heavily upon her.

She had no right to be jealous, none at all.

The tears that had surprised her yesterday surged to the surface. She desperately fought them back. What had happened to her discipline of late?

"You look beautiful tonight," he said. "What have you done to your hair?"

"I had it cut and highlighted." She lifted her chin and waited for him to chide her for going to the beauty salon.

He merely raised his eyebrows. "Very nice."

Disarmed by the compliment, she tried to inject

an air of graciousness in her manner. After all, he was a guest and this was her mother's house. She was aware of her mother's anxious gaze several times during the meal.

"The garden is lovely," Kate told them after they ate. "I think I'll serve coffee and dessert on the patio. You young people go on out."

Susan stifled a groan. Outside, she led the way to an old-fashioned swing and several padded chairs on a flagstone patio. A trellis formed an alcove for the swing. Enclosing the alcove in a bower of sweet scent, honeysuckle climbed the cedar slats overhead.

The moon hung like a silver shield as the sky darkened into deep dusk. A few fireflies were visible in the field behind the house.

"Sit," Michael said, taking her hand and urging her toward the swing.

She went reluctantly, not wanting to make a to-do about something unimportant. Sitting, she realized how tired she was. She'd walked, caught up the ranch books on the computer for her father, then prepared lunch since it was Esperanza's day off. Restless, she'd walked again that afternoon, down by the creek where she and Michael had kissed so passionately.

When they were seated side by side, Michael started the swing gliding back and forth. "Your mother will be pleased to see us like this," he murmured, laughter in his tone.

She was aware of his heat next to her. She wanted to lean into it and let it warm her all the way through. She'd never felt so down, so filled with grief.

"I'm not an introspective person," she said, then sighed. "I'm not usually unhappy. It isn't something I really think about."

"But you are now?"

The depth of his voice soothed her, like honey melting on toast. "I don't know. There's no reason to be. I know you warned me about depression, and I'm not depressed." She heard how insistent she sounded. "Maybe I am."

"If you could have anything you wished, what would you want different in your life?"

She half turned so she could study his face in the last rays of twilight. "I'd want to dance again."

He nodded. "What else?"

Pressing her hands together, she realized they were cold. She'd gotten used to cold hands and feet with her old heart, but since the operation, she'd not experienced it. She remembered how the air around them had heated up when they'd made love.

"You," she whispered.

With a finger under her chin, he urged her head around until he could see into her eyes. "Do you think you're safe saying that now, while we're at your mother's house?"

His eyes blazed with passion, devouring her with

their mutual hunger. Fire rushed along her veins, and she was suddenly very warm.

She shook her head, moving away from him and his magic touch. "I don't know why I said that. Lately I seem to have lost control over my emo— my tongue. I never had that problem when I was performing."

"Your dancer's discipline," he said, understanding. "You'll be able to dance again."

"Not as prima," she denied. "Have you ever seen *Swan Lake?* It's the most demanding role in ballet."

"I saw you in it. Every man in the audience was in love with you by the end."

"Including you?" She smiled, her troubled spirits suddenly soothed.

"Especially me."

He laid an arm on the swing behind her, enclosing her in the safety of his embrace. His lips were fixed in a half smile, as if he watched her dance on the stage of memory.

"I miss it—the practice, the anticipation before the curtain goes up, the excitement when the music starts and you're carried onto the stage by the notes. You feel as if you can fly."

She realized she'd lifted her arms in the graceful beat of the swan and let them fall back into her lap, once more swamped by the nostalgia, or whatever it was that plagued her.

"You can do it again if that's what you really

want,'' he promised. ''You have only to believe in yourself.''

''I've tried. The stamina is gone.'' She glared at him when he laughed.

''Impatient little swan,'' he murmured, trailing a finger down her cheek. ''You'll have to work up to it, but you can get there again.''

For a moment, she believed him.

Her mother came outside, carrying a tray. Michael rose to help her with it. ''Have you bought tickets yet for the Harvest Moon Ball?'' she asked him. ''It's next Saturday. The proceeds go to improvements in the city park.''

He looked at Susan. ''I'll take two.''

''Wonderful,'' Kate said. ''I happen to have them right here.''

''Will you be my date?'' he asked Susan.

Kate looked from one to the other, her eyes alight.

''I'm not supposed to be in crowds,'' Susan reminded him.

''I'll make the other men keep their distance.''

Looking at his determined face and her mother's happy one, Susan sighed and gave in. ''I'd be delighted.''

''There,'' Kate told her. ''That didn't hurt a bit, did it?''

Michael chuckled as she cast her mother a reproachful glance. Then, unable to help it, she smiled, too.

Eleven

Michael yawned as he pulled into the garage at his house. He noticed a light in the kitchen and figured he'd left it on.

He didn't expect the Mafia men to be visiting. The news on the car radio had announced Carmine Mercado's funeral was scheduled for Tuesday. He didn't plan to attend. That was where he drew the line with his patients.

Entering the house warily, he heard music and relaxed. "Hello?" he called.

"Uncle Michael," his niece yelled from the kitchen.

She appeared, all arms and legs and mane of straight black hair swinging down to her waist, and threw herself into his arms, sobbing.

He patted her back and held her until the weeping fit subsided. "A fight with the parents?"

She shook her head. "Not exactly. Rafe and I've broken up. He was with someone else. Marilyn Karr."

Janis and Rafe had been steadies since tenth grade in high school, but the relationship had been rife with problems since she'd gone off to college. He vaguely recalled that the other girl was his niece's archenemy and had wanted Rafe from the very first.

"He wanted me to move in with him, but Mom and Dad said no. Now he's found someone else."

Michael refrained from saying this sounded like a good thing to him. "Perhaps you misunderstood the situation."

She pulled away and stalked about the living room. "Ha! I found them in bed Sunday morning. She'd spent the night with him. I'll never forgive him."

"It does look bad," he agreed. "A man who can't be trusted is no kind of man."

"Exactly." She plopped down on the sofa. "I can't stand school anymore. I thought I'd stay with you while I figure out where to go from here." She cast him an anxious plea from her light-blue eyes that contrasted sharply with her hair and deep tan. Her Asian heritage, from her mother, was evident in the almond shape of her eyes.

"As long as you let your parents know where you are, it's okay with me. Have you called them?"

She hesitated, then shook her head.

"Do it now, then we'll talk."

An idea had come to him. If Janis was still interested in ballet, maybe Susan could advise her. He poured a glass of tea while Janis spoke to her father, then she handed the phone to him. Michael talked to

Jim and Mona, assuring them he didn't mind taking Janis in while things calmed down.

"I'd like her to keep away from Rafe," Jim said. "Could she stay in Houston with you for a while?"

"I don't see why not. I'd be delighted for her to stay at the condo. Until we get her transferred, I'll put her to work catching up on the filing in my office."

"Good. She needs to be kept busy."

Michael grimaced at the stern tone but said nothing. He didn't mention the ballet or Susan. This wasn't the right time. Besides which, his idea might come to nothing. After he hung up, he studied his niece.

"Well?" she demanded.

"You can stay."

She squealed and gave him a bear hug. "I'll be so quiet, you won't know I'm in the place," she promised.

"Good. You can start by turning off that music. If you have to listen to it, do so in your room."

"No problem." She turned off the TV music channel. "Would you like to listen to the late news?"

"No, thanks. I'm beat. See you in the morning." But it was a long time before he fell asleep. His mind seethed with plans that might or might not work.

The first person Susan saw when she walked onto the café patio at the country club Monday was Michael. She started guiltily and had to forcefully suppress an inclination to run before he saw her.

Too late. His narrowed blue-eyed gaze followed her across the granite flagstones to her friend's table.

Not only was she in a public place, but she wasn't wearing a mask. However, she had requested a table on the patio on the theory that the open air would be better for her than being confined inside. She lifted her chin and smiled coolly at him.

He gave her a casual nod and grinned, then he turned back to the beautiful woman with him.

Something hot and primitive hit Susan in the solar plexus. For a second, she wanted to go over and hit him.

On a second perusal, though, she realized the woman with him was young and, judging from her black hair, blue eyes and tawny skin, might be kin to him. There was definitely a resemblance.

"Susan, you're here. You look great. How do you feel?" Darla, a friend from first grade, asked.

"Fine. How's the family?"

Darla, voted the most likely to succeed in their class, had married right out of high school. She and her husband owned a construction and paving business. They had two kids.

"Growing like weeds. I brought pictures." She dug them out of an oversize purse.

Susan enjoyed the stories about her friend's seven-year-old son and five-year-old daughter as they chatted without pause during the meal. An hour and a half later, Darla looked at the time and leaped to her feet. "Got to run. It's time to pick up Kailyn at kindergarten. It was wonderful seeing you. Call when you have time."

Susan watched her friend rush for the parking lot. Darla's life seemed so full and rich in ways that counted. Husband, kids, successful business. Some people had it all.

Watching three golfers finish the eighteenth hole, she felt the emptiness in her own life. Since Michael seemed to think there was no reason she couldn't go back to the stage, she'd started a very restrained practice program that morning. It made her feel better to be doing something constructive, to have a *plan* for her life.

She wondered if it would be enough. What more could she possibly want? Nothing came to mind.

Hearing footsteps, she glanced around. Michael and his lunch companion were approaching. Her spine stiffened.

"Hi, mind if we intrude?" he asked. "I wanted you to meet someone."

"Please, join me," she invited, her eyes on the young woman, who had the most perfect features she'd ever seen.

"Janis, this is Susan Wainwright," he said, holding a chair for the young woman. "Susan, this is my niece. Janis is visiting from Hawaii. She's going to stay with me for a while.''

Before Susan had time to sort through the implications of his remarks, his niece's eyes opened wide. "Not *the* Susan Wainwright?" she said incredulously. "The prima with the Houston Ballet?"

"Well, I was once upon a time," Susan said lightly. "I'm more or less retired at present." She flicked a glance at Michael, who had taken the chair to her right. "Until your uncle says it's okay, I can't go back."

The girl cast a puzzled look at Michael.

"Susan had heart replacement surgery last month," he explained. "She's recovering nicely."

"Oh, good."

Susan felt a bit uncomfortable being the center of such evident hero worship. She wasn't sure what to say.

Michael spoke up. "Janis is interested in ballet. How does one go about auditioning for the Houston company?"

"No, no," Janis protested, a blush rising to her cheeks. "I'm not good enough."

"How do you know?" Susan asked. "Have you tried?"

Janis lowered her head. "I didn't get into Julliard two years ago."

"It's a tough school. Have you been practicing since?"

"Yes, and taking lessons while going to the university. My parents insist I get a teaching certificate so I can support myself."

"They have a point," Susan agreed. "The arts are very competitive. Even if you're good enough, it may not be sufficient. Being in the right place at the right time may be impossible."

"If she danced for you, would you be willing to evaluate her?" Michael asked.

Put on the spot, Susan nodded slowly.

"No!" Janis said, obviously aghast at the idea. "I couldn't impose like that. But thank you anyway. I saw a video of you in *The Nutcracker*. My ballet teacher showed it to the class last Christmas." She sighed. "I would love to dance in that setting. It was wonderful. How did you ever do that leap from the balcony into the Nutcracker's arms?"

Before Susan quite knew how it happened, she was deep into details of the various ballets she'd performed. Janis's interest was unwavering as she asked endless questions about movements, costumes and settings.

Michael's eyes shifted from one to the other as he silently listened. At times, he watched duffers on the last hole, a slight smile on his lips. Susan wondered what he was thinking.

She suspected some kind of conspiracy, but ruled that out. Janis was too transparent to take part. However, Michael wasn't above taking advantage of any situation that arose. When Janis excused herself and left them, Susan turned to him. "Is this your way of introducing the idea of teaching to me?"

He wasn't the least bit nonplussed by the blunt question. "I thought it was a possibility. Is it working?"

She shrugged. "Your niece is a true lover of the form. I'd like to see her dance."

"You'll have to convince her."

She nodded as a tingle of excitement buzzed through her. The company needed new blood. It would be nice to discover a fresh talent for them. Pausing, she studied Michael for a long moment.

"What?" he asked.

"I like her, but I don't like the idea of being manipulated. Is this part of your therapy for patients?"

He shrugged, his expression harsh. "Sometimes I'd like to pound some sense into you."

She stood. "I'll call Janis. Will you be here or in Houston?"

"Here the rest of the week, back in Houston Monday morning."

Nodding, she left the café and drove back to the ranch. Going to her room, she repeated her short routine of ballet movements and exercises designed to keep her muscles flexible while she recovered.

Afterward, resting, she supposed it was only human to feel envious of a younger, healthier rival, but she didn't like the feeling. However, she was enthusiastic about helping Janis. Watching the girl's graceful movements, she'd spotted talent. It just needed to be developed more fully.

Susan watched Janis with a critical eye. "Lift," she said. "Higher. You're a little sloppy. Always lift the leg a bit higher before you put it down, as if it's so effortless, you could do much more."

Janis nodded. She blotted sweat from her forehead on the sleeve of her red leotard and lifted her leg again, held it for the next two beats, lifted it a couple more inches, then dropped it gracefully to the floor.

Susan didn't like the red leotard. Her own teacher at Juillard had insisted on black for practice. Always.

Funny how habits became ingrained, and how it ruffled one's sense of propriety for them to be disturbed.

The two had been working together for three days. Janis had a mind of her own about interpreting the ballet. There was a sense of creativity about her that was refreshing. Susan again experienced the thrill of discovery.

"Okay, that's enough," she said. "Here's your uncle."

"Already?" Janis looked at her watch, obviously amazed at how swiftly the afternoon had flown.

Susan was pleased. It was another sign of a dedicated dancer. "Use my shower, if you like, before you change. I'll keep him entertained."

"Michael," Janis said suddenly, giving Susan a keen look. "His name is Michael."

"Uh, yes." Susan started for the door.

"You don't call him by name unless you have to. Why is that? Don't you like him?"

"Well, of course. Your unc—Michael is a very nice person." She put a slight emphasis on the name to show it didn't bother her to use it.

Unbidden, an image came to her. The two of them in his bed, her murmuring his name over and over...

She pressed her lips together as her breath came fast and her heart stampeded.

Laughing, Janis headed for the bathroom.

Susan went to the front porch to greet Michael. She'd seen him every day that week, once when he delivered Janis to the ranch for their practice sessions and again when he picked her up. Although he stayed but a moment each time, his presence lingered long after he had driven off to meet his friends at the golf links.

Her sister, Rose, knew quite a bit about Michael due to his friendship with the Carson family. Susan had picked up odd pieces of information. He was one of the best golfers of their group. He preferred iced tea as his regular drink, raspberry flavored being his favorite. He was considered easygoing and affable.

Apparently no one thought he was arrogant but her.

But then, maybe he didn't try to interfere in his friends' lives, only hers. And maybe Janis's, but only in a very positive manner.

"How's it going?" he asked.

A white cowboy hat shaded his eyes. He was dressed in navy shorts, a white polo shirt and tennis shoes. It wasn't fair that he could look so incredibly handsome day after day. Her breath hung in her throat so that she had to clear it before she could speak.

"Fine. I want to arrange an audition for Janis with the ballet director and choreographer."

His face became serious. "Really?"

"Really. She's wonderful, a bit headstrong, but creative and dedicated. I think she can make it."

The smile returned. "Headstrong. Now who else do I know like that?" He pretended to think about it.

Susan poked him in the ribs. "Very funny."

When he caught her hand and gave a tug, she teetered forward. He wrapped her in his arms. "Thanks for taking her on. I thought she was good the last time I saw her dance, but I'm no judge. Mmm, you smell good."

Putting her hands on his chest, instead of pushing away, she lingered in his embrace. She glanced up into his eyes and was hooked. Neither looked away.

"Could I get another ticket for the ball Saturday night? I don't want to leave Janis home by herself."

She nodded.

"How are you feeling?" he asked, finally stepping back. "Can you lift your arms above shoulder level?"

"Yes."

"Show me."

So there on the porch, she performed the exercise routine she'd devised to keep her in shape. He nodded and approved each one and extolled her determination to get past the pain of the surgery. When she finished, he swiped a finger across her forehead.

"You didn't even break a sweat," he complimented. His eyes roamed her face. "You're my miracle patient, the one I hold up as an example for others to emulate."

"I don't feel like a good example. It's taking forever to get back to where I was—"

She stopped in surprise when he burst into laughter.

"You don't know," he chided huskily. "You haven't a clue. It takes a full year for most people to get back to where they were before any surgery, much less the one you had. You expect to be there in what, not quite five weeks? It's amazing that you can lift each arm to shoulder height and above."

"I won't be an invalid," she told him.

His smile softened. "Even if you were in a wheelchair, you wouldn't be an invalid. You're a fighter, one of the bravest I've ever met. Ah, here's my niece.''

Janis bounded out of the house.

''Susan tells me you're headstrong and willful. I explained you were merely spoiled,'' he teased.

''I'm sure you misunderstood. She told *me* I was talented and creative,'' the girl retorted.

Susan laughed at their play as she waved them off. Watching Michael with his relative that week, she'd realized what a good man he was and what a wonderful father he would make. Thinking of Darla's adorable children, she thought of the children Michael would someday have.

He was ready for a home and family. His buying the house was proof, according to her mother and grandmother. They'd advised her to snap him up.

Pressing a hand to her chest to contain the sudden tumult of feeling there, she wondered what kind of life she could really live. Perhaps she should check the Internet and see what other transplant patients said.

Janis pressed a hand to her stomach. ''I'm so nervous,'' she confided. ''I can't remember anything.''

Michael patted her shoulder. ''Once you're on the stage, the music will guide you.'' He hoped that was true.

Susan came backstage. ''Okay, we're ready. Remember, keep those lifts high and effortless. Focus on that."

"Right. Lifts high."

"Go," Susan ordered.

Janis walked out and stood before the blinding footlights. She struck a pose. The music began.

"I'm more nervous than she is," Susan admitted. "Being a teacher is harder than one would suppose."

Michael clasped her hand and found it was cold. He brought it to his lips and pressed a kiss on each finger. "She'll do fine. Wow," he said as Janis made her first leap.

"Now, glissade, glissade," Susan whispered. "Oh, very good. Perfect jeté."

He was content to hold Susan's hand and watch his niece perform her piece. He had flown the three of them to Houston that morning. They would spend the night in town, then fly back tomorrow for the Harvest Moon Ball.

If the audition didn't work out, Janis had already called the university about transferring her credits and starting classes next quarter. She'd decided to be a dance teacher if she couldn't be a prima ballerina.

Susan clapped and rushed forward when the music ended. She gave Janis a hug and told her to wait backstage while she talked to the director and choreographer. In a few minutes she returned, her eyes sparkling.

"They agreed with my assessment." She turned

to Janis. "If you're willing to work very, very hard, they're willing to sign you on."

"You mean...will I dance in the chorus?" Janis asked, her cheeks aflame with excitement.

Susan laughed and shook her head. "You'll start in small parts, of course, but you'll be groomed for prima."

Janis clutched her chest. "I think I'm having a heart attack, Uncle Michael."

He linked an arm through hers and Susan's arms. "Come on. Let's go home. We all need to relax."

At the penthouse, they settled on the balcony overlooking the city and discussed the younger woman's possible career. He was content to listen.

Life seemed sweet at the moment. His two girls were happy. That was all that mattered to him. He looked from Janis to Susan. A fierce protective pride rose in him, a feeling like none other that he had ever experienced.

His girls?

Yes, in all the ways that counted.

When the phone rang, he went to answer. A man asked for Janis. "I'll get her. Is this Rafe?"

"Uh, yeah."

Janis sucked in a surprised breath when he told her who was on the line, then her expression changed, becoming thoughtful. "That seems so long ago. Another time, another place. Rafe is the past," she told Michael.

"I suggest you tell him that."

When she went to her room to take the call, he settled in his chair with a worried frown.

"She'll be okay," Susan said.

"Rafe has been around a long time. I've never understood the attraction myself, but Janis seems pretty loyal to him."

"Maybe he was part of a rebellion against her parents. Free of that, she'll be free of him. She's on the right track now."

He heaved a breath of relief. "You've been good to her. Have I told you how much I appreciate it?"

"She's been a joy to work with." She gazed into the distance, a slight smile playing at the corners of her mouth.

His heart contracted in a painful spasm. He'd never felt this way around a woman, aroused yet content.

"Remind me to take my tux for the ball tomorrow night," he requested.

"I've been wondering if I should go."

He gave her a lazily threatening glare. "I'll come out and dress you myself if you try to welsh on the deal. Come to think of it, that sounds like an excellent idea."

She returned his grin, but her eyes were thoughtful. For a moment he wondered if his plans for tomorrow night would come to fruition. Quite simply, he planned to seduce the willful ballerina.

Janis returned and took her seat. "That was Rafe," she said. "He wants me to come home." She burst into tears.

Michael cursed silently, not sure what to do.

Susan moved over to Janis. With a hand, she gestured for him to leave them alone.

Feeling every bit the coward that he was, he beat a hasty retreat to the study. Some matters of the heart were better left to other experts.

Twelve

Susan looked over the few formal outfits she kept at the ranch. Nothing seemed exactly right. She wanted something new and different, something no one had ever seen. Something that would be special for M—for the evening.

Irritated with her indecision, she grabbed a sea-green chiffon silk that floated around her ankles. The matching jacket had bugle beads sparkling all over it. This would do just fine.

Slipping into the silk underdress, she paused and looked at herself in the full-length mirror. The scar started just below the hollow of her throat and flowed down to the end of her breastbone. An orderly row of dots from the stitches punctuated each side of it.

Most of the fiery redness was gone. The stitches were already fading. Michael had said they would go away with time and the long scar would become a faint white line.

Thinking of his caresses there, she realized the scar didn't bother him at all. It hadn't lessened his desire for her. His kisses were still as hot, as passionate as before. The imperfection didn't bother her, either. She didn't feel ugly or any less a woman.

Because of him.

Well, not entirely. But it was no big thing to him, just a fact of life, and so she looked at herself the same way. The surgery had been necessary. A few scars were part of the cure. Life was like that.

She inhaled deeply, letting the truth flow into that place where hopes and dreams dwelled.

Suddenly the future lay before her like the magical yellow brick road to Oz. The dizziness, shortness of breath and chest pains were entirely gone. The explosive ticking of her undersized heart had ended, replaced by the steady beat of a young, healthy heart. Tears blurred her vision.

Thank you for this chance, she said to the young woman who, in death, had given of herself so that others might live. Michael would know the girl's name.

"If I have a child," she whispered, bowing her head, "it'll be for you, for this gift of life."

Quickly, with time running short, she slipped into the light green silk, then applied makeup, adding a golden shine to her eyelids and cheeks. Tonight, she felt like a golden girl.

After fastening a gold chain around her neck and dangly earrings in her ears, she slipped into the jacket and headed for the door just as she heard Michael's car in the driveway.

"You look beautiful," her father said, meeting her at the door to welcome Michael.

"And you look handsome enough to be a prince," she told Archy.

He did look nice in his tux, the silver of his hair shining like treasure. Her green eyes, as well as Justin's, came from him while Rose had her mother's violet-blue eyes. Love rushed over her all at once, and she gave him a fierce hug, feeling the loneliness in him.

"Are you picking up Mother?" she asked.

"No. I offered, but she had to go in early. She's on the decorating committee."

The doorbell rang.

Taking a deep breath, Susan opened the door to Michael…and caught her breath.

"Wow," she murmured. "I'm not sure my heart can handle the two handsomest men in the world at the same time."

"Flattery will get you anywhere you want to go," Michael said with a sexy laugh.

"Good to see you, Michael," Archy greeted him and shook hands with him.

"Would you like a lift to the club?" Michael asked. "My niece is with me, but we have room for one more."

"No, no. You young people run along. I'll be there soon."

After they were out the door, Susan said softly, "I think he's lonely. I wish he and Mother..."

"Would get back together?" Michael finished for her.

"Yes." She sighed. "I'm in an odd mood, nostalgic and wishful and happy and sad. Does that make sense?"

"It doesn't have to," he assured her, opening the door and helping her into the seat.

She said hello to Janis, sitting in the back.

"You look gorgeous," the younger woman said. "Uncle Michael took me shopping this afternoon. I found a nice dress, but nothing as lovely as yours."

Susan still found it difficult to be the center of hero worship. "The black outfit goes beautifully with your hair. Your eyes are a knockout."

"I'm a lucky man," Michael boasted. "Two beautiful women and both with me."

"We're lucky too," Janis added. "The tux makes you look older and very distinguished."

"Older, huh?" Michael winked at Susan. "I don't know whether I've been insulted or not."

"Not at all. Your arrogance would never allow it."

"Now I *know* I've been insulted."

Susan smiled while uncle and niece continued their raillery. The odd mixture of emotion rolled over her again. Tonight she wanted something different. She glanced at her escort. Him. She wanted him.

"Who is that?" Janis demanded when they arrived at the country club entrance.

The doorman helped the ladies out while Michael gave the keys to the valet. Susan followed Janis's wide-eyed gaze. She studied the unsmiling man who, while dressed formally, looked as untamed as a wolf.

"Hawk Wainwright," she said.

"He's kin to you? Can you introduce us?" Janis asked.

Susan looked at Michael, who shrugged. She wasn't sure if she should put an innocent like Janis in the company of a loner like Hawk. "Yes," she finally said, "but a prima doesn't have time for relationships, not while she's getting established."

Janis sighed. "I know, but he's so gorgeous. Oh, he's looking this way. Maybe he'll ask me to dance later."

Susan smiled at Hawk, a man she thought was her half brother, although her father had never admitted it.

He nodded politely, but without smiling back, although he didn't frown, either. The man would be great at playing poker, she thought.

Once inside, they went up the elevator to the ballroom and through the receiving line, which was headed by Susan's mother, then they joined Rose and Matt, Josie and Flynt at a table. Susan was surprised at how natural it felt to be with the Carson brothers. She even smiled at Fiona and Cara Carson, who were at a nearby table, although a tiny flash of something like jealousy did dart through her. The twins were lovely.

Glancing at Michael, she experienced an increasing glow inside. Tonight, she promised her buoyant spirits, tonight she was going to be with him.

"Hey, I'm glad I caught you guys," a man she didn't know said, coming to their table.

Flynt jumped to his feet. "Ben, good to see you. Join us. We have an extra chair."

"I'm circulating," the other man said.

Flynt introduced the stranger. "This is Ben Ashton. He's investigating Lena's background for us. Have you found out anything about her parents?"

The private investigator grimaced. "I know Tyler isn't the father. His DNA doesn't come close to the baby's."

"That leaves Luke," Flynt said with a frown. "Where the heck is he?"

The other two golfing buddies arrived and heard this last remark. "Probably some tropical island with his latest conquest," Tyler suggested irritably.

Spence spoke up. "This time ol' Luke must be smitten. He's been gone for months."

"And probably has had a different girl for each one of them," Tyler added.

Flynt laughed. "Tyler's jealous. He was in love with Haley Mercado when we were kids. She only had eyes for Luke."

Tyler was good-natured about the teasing. "Yeah, but you were half in love with her, too."

"A mere boyhood crush," Flynt assured his friend.

Susan, watching the play among the men, thought Flynt Carson had never looked more relaxed. There was a quiet happiness about him and Josie, also between Rose and Matt, that spoke of promises made and kept.

Emotion grabbed at her heart and wouldn't let go. She wanted what they had.

"Shall we dance?" Michael asked.

She realized the music had started. But no one was on the dance floor yet, which sent a nervous tremor through her.

"Come," he urged, standing and holding out his hand.

She was aware of other eyes on her. Reluctantly she let herself be escorted to the center of the ballroom floor. Her breath keep snagging in her throat, filling it with a lump of dread. She hadn't danced in front of anyone since her collapse onstage. She wasn't sure she could.

Michael took her hand. She laid the other on his shoulder. As he moved, she felt the strength in him. His warmth surrounded her in a net of safety.

Looking into his eyes, she found she could breathe after all. And dance.

They swayed and dipped to the beautiful strains

of the waltz, their steps perfectly matched. The room faded, and they were alone, surrounded by the glow of a thousand candles and a magical enchantment all their own.

Tonight, her heart sang. She would share passion with him tonight and not worry about what tomorrow would bring.

She gazed into his eyes and couldn't look away. When the dance ended, silence surrounded them, then sound reached her ears, soft at first, then louder and louder.

Startled, Susan peered around the huge room. School chums, friends, people she'd known all her life stood and applauded, their faces wreathed in smiles. She saw her father pull his handkerchief from his pocket and hand it to her mother, who hastily wiped her eyes.

"Take a bow, vixen," Michael said softly.

Her own eyes filling with tears, Susan dropped into a deep curtsy, her hand still securely in his. With her other hand, she blew kisses to each corner of the ballroom, feeling the love and wealth of good wishes that accompanied the salute. Then Michael escorted her to the table.

"You two were magnificent!" Janis exclaimed. "You could make it on the ballroom dancing professional circuit."

"No, thanks. Dancing is harder than heart surgery," Michael said with obvious sincerity.

That drew a laugh from the others and started tales among the men of their first terrifying dancing experiences.

At the side of the room, Susan spied Hawk standing in solitary splendor, his eyes taking in everything, giving away nothing. She couldn't bear for anyone to be left out tonight. "Go ask him to dance," she whispered to Janis.

Janis bit her lip as she stared at the dark, silent outsider. "Do I dare?"

Susan nodded. "A flirtation only," she warned. "No serious involvement for five years. Invite him to join us. He can have the extra chair."

Michael raised his eyebrows at this suggestion, but kept silent. His eyes conveyed his trust in Susan's judgment.

"He must always feel left out," Janis murmured.

"Be careful that he doesn't see your pity. He wouldn't like it," Michael whispered back, then watched his niece thread her way across the room.

Susan held her breath as Janis stopped in front of Hawk and hoped he wouldn't hurt the young woman's feelings. However, he appeared to be listening in his grave way, then he shook hands with her. Janis glanced toward the dance floor, then back to Hawk.

Susan clutched Michael's hand.

Hawk took Janis's elbow and led the way to the

dance floor. They joined the other couples who swayed to a slow, dreamy love song.

Susan sighed in relief.

"Tender heart," Michael accused.

"Hey, there's Frank Del Brio," Matt said, nodding toward the door.

"Johnny and Ricky Mercado are with him. Who's the woman with Ricky?" Flynt wanted to know.

"I don't know her," Susan said. She watched the foursome join two other couples at a table. "They don't like each other, Ricky and Frank. They're as stiff as two cats about to have a fight."

"One of them will take Carmine's place," Michael observed. "Which one?"

"My bet's on Frank," Flynt said, laying a five on the table.

"You're covered," Matt declared, taking a five out of his wallet. "Ricky won't take orders from a punk like Frank. He's too independent."

Michael laid his money on the table. "My bet is on Spence. He'll shut down their operations within the year."

Flynt swept up the three bills. "Here, Josie, hold the bets. At the New Year's ball, we'll see who wins."

"And who loses," Michael said.

All eyes were on the three men who were now the tentative leaders of the Texas Mafia: Johnny Mercado, eldest and brother to the late don; Ricky Mercado, nephew and chosen heir; Frank Del Brio, rumored to be ruthless and powerful and determined to be the new don.

Susan shivered as a sense of evil wafted around her. Michael, sensitive to her moods, laid an arm around her shoulders as if to protect her.

"Tonight," she murmured, basking in his strong presence that drove out all other thought.

He gave her a startled glance, then his eyes warmed as flames leaped in them. "Tonight," he echoed.

She didn't know what they had agreed to, but she was going to take whatever fate offered.

Tonight, tonight, her heart sang in its own rendition of *West Side Story*.

When Hawk brought the beaming Janis back to the table, Susan asked him to join them. Rose gave her a startled glance, then seconded the invitation.

Hawk looked them over gravely, smiled, then took the empty chair next to Janis. "It looks as if everyone in the county is here tonight, doesn't it?"

Susan followed his glance to where her father stood, talking to the mayor and Spence Harrison. A bit farther along the room, her mother was chatting to another member of the committee who had planned the ball and its elaborate display of fall flowers. Pity ate at her. She wanted everyone to share the magic tonight.

"It isn't your fault," Michael said for her ears only.

"I know, but—"

"Come on," he said suddenly. "Let's get out of here."

Too startled to protest, she rose when he did.

"Would you see Janis home?" he asked Hawk.

The man nodded. Janis pressed a hand to her chest. The two married couples looked on without a word.

"Good. Susan has had enough tonight. She's not supposed to be in crowds at all for another two months," he said sternly, then spoiled it by smiling indulgently.

Susan bid them all good-night and silently followed Michael from the room. When the valet brought the car around and they were off, her new heart skipped an alarming number of beats. She went weak and dizzy, but there was no pain, no pain at all. Only the most intense excitement she'd ever known.

"Tonight," she said.

"Yes."

At Michael's home on Mission Ridge, Susan took his hand and let him help her out of the sports car and into the house. She expected an offer of champagne or wine or at least his favorite tipple—raspberry iced tea.

Instead she was enfolded in strong arms the moment they entered the dim foyer. "Mmm-hmm," she said, clutching his strong shoulders and giving herself to the kiss.

Rockets blazed inside her. They roared in her ears so that all she could hear over the sound was the fast beating of her heart. His lips roamed hers in tender forays, then became more demanding. She opened to his bidding and played a lover's eternal game of touch and retreat.

"I want you," she told him, pushing the tux jacket off and down his arms. "Now. Oh, Michael, *now*."

He lifted his head and stared into her eyes, the look in his causing her knees to go weak.

"Not yet," he said in a ragged voice.

Releasing his hold, he turned them toward the living room and flicked on soft lamplight before seating her on the sofa. She gazed at him, questions in her eyes and uncertainty in her soul, while he sat on the edge of the chair, his knees an inch from hers. He leaned forward, an intensity in him she'd seen just before her surgery.

"We need to talk," he continued.

"Why?" she asked softly, teasing him with a deliberate, flirty under-the-lashes look.

He sucked in a deep breath. "Vixen. Don't distract me. Tell me what you want."

She almost laughed. "You."

But Michael was serious, dead serious. He knew

what he wanted from her and wouldn't settle for less. "You got me, lady, lock, stock, and barrel."

Her eyes glowed, drowning him in their brilliance and the simmering sexuality in her glance. He forced himself to think instead of only feel.

"It has to be forever," he added, making his position clear. He'd come to that realization weeks ago. Observing the wariness enter her eyes now, he was sure she hadn't thought that far ahead.

"Forever is a long time," she said, not meeting his eyes. "We might not have that long."

"True, but whatever time there is, I want it."

She smiled again. "Me, too. Can we start now?"

He shook his head in frustration. He was sure they weren't on the same wavelength. "I'm talking about marriage, Susan," he said bluntly, putting his heart on the line. "I want that kind of forever."

Susan's mood changed at once. She rose and paced to the broad expanse of windows. She could see the harvest moon shining on the lake, a huge golden pumpkin that could turn into a coach with the wave of a magic wand.

Only it wouldn't. Not for her.

"Don't spoil things," she pleaded.

He came to her and laid his wonderful hands on her shoulders, his chest against her back, creating a blanket of warmth around her. She refrained from leaning into him.

"How would marriage do that? I'm in love with

you. That's a forever kind of thing as far as I'm concerned.''

Tears pressed in harsh waves against her control. She sought and found the anger. Spinning away from him, she said in a low, fierce tone, ''There's no such thing as forever for us. I have tonight. That's all I can guarantee.''

He studied her through narrowed eyes, his handsome face set in hard lines. She fought the hateful tears.

''I'll take tonight,'' he said.

She crossed her arms over her chest, fighting the sweet caress of his voice, so deep and midnight dark and enticing.

''But I'm a selfish bastard. I want all your nights and your days. I'm talking about commitment. Can you give me that?''

Despair battled the anger. ''No.''

Michael started to reach for her, to shake some sense into her pretty head, but he forced his hands to his sides. It was hard, but a man had to know when he was wrong.

''So it was gratitude,'' he murmured, more to himself than her. ''The doctor-patient syndrome.''

She stared out the window, refusing to meet his gaze. Her hands clenched and unclenched at her sides. ''You know it was more.''

He laughed sardonically. ''Yeah, sex. That part was great, but frankly, the rest of our relationship has been hell. Come on, I'll take you home. You look pale."

"Michael," Susan whispered, and heard the agony in her voice.

He stiffened and waited.

"Please, don't send me away."

"There's only so much I can take, Susan. I think I've reached the end of my rope tonight."

She swallowed the knot of misery. "I know the chances of survival. This next year is critical. It could be all I'll have. A year, a few months, maybe weeks, or only days. Who can say? I feel good now, but that could change at any time."

"Don't you think I know that? I'm asked to calculate the mortality of my patients all the time. I want forever, however long that may be."

She shook her head. "It would hurt too much...to want so much and perhaps have so little."

"I have a friend from medical school," he told her. "He had a kidney transplant when he was fifteen. He's alive and has a busy family practice. He has a wife and kid. He takes two pills a day. That's it."

She wanted to marry him, she wanted to dance again, she wanted to coach other young dancers and see them blossom, she wanted two children. Dear God, she wanted to believe it was all possible. But she didn't.

Her watch vibrated against her wrist. "Time for the pills," she said dully, and reached for her purse.

Michael brought her a glass of water. After she swallowed the dozen pills that kept her heart and body from rejecting each other, he simply watched her for a moment, then he laughed with a bitterness that shook her soul.

"I thought you were brave," he said. "I thought you could face the future, that you would grab it and make it your own. I thought you would share it with me."

"I will, but not— I don't think it's necessary to marry. We can date and do things together."

"Not good enough. I want you with me every day. I want to fall asleep with you in my arms, wake with you in my bed. I want to think about children and whether we should try for one or adopt one a couple of years from now."

"You are so stubborn," she accused, seeing only darkness ahead if he wouldn't agree to her terms.

"Yeah, I am. Just like someone else I know. This is a hell of a note, isn't it? You want limited involvement and no commitment. I want it all." He sighed. "Let's go."

Panic seized her. "No! Give me time to think." She pressed fingertips to her temples. "You're a doctor. You know everything."

He snorted at this.

"Everything about me," she clarified. "And you still want marriage?

He nodded.

A hum started inside her, spreading outward like the vibrating notes of the violins denoting the change of mood at a tense moment in a ballet.

"I could die," she said.

Silence.

"I don't want to be a burden. I'd hate that."

Silence.

"Can't you just sweep me off my feet and override all my worries and objections?" she cried.

Silence.

She huffed out a breath and took a step forward. Then another one. "You could help, you know," she told him.

He raised his eyebrows in that lofty, arrogant way she loved. Her heart pounded fiercely.

Another step. There was only one left between them. She stopped and looked into his eyes. She saw laughter and warmth and delight. She saw tenderness and caring and nurturing. She saw love.

"I love you," she said, giving in to it. "Marriage it is, but if you're ever sorry, don't say I didn't tell you so."

He threw back his head and laughed. Then he swept her into his arms. Her evening slippers fell off. He kicked them out of the way as he turned toward the hall.

She snuggled her head on his shoulder and kissed his neck and jaw and cheek as far as she could reach. He strode the length of the house to the master bedroom.

Stopping in the middle of the floor, where moonlight flooded the carpet in a silver square of enchantment, she felt as if they had walked into a new world, a place made for them and their love.

"As long as we're here," she murmured, "in this magic place of love, we'll be safe."

"You'll always be safe with me," he promised huskily. "We're going to be so content, each moment will seem like a special forever, created just for us."

She believed him.

Don't miss the next story from
Silhouette's

LONE STAR COUNTRY CLUB:
PROMISED TO A SHEIK
by Carla Cassidy

Available October 2002
(ISBN:0-373-61356-3)

Turn the page for an excerpt from this
exciting romance…!

One

"Sheik Al Abdar, could you tell us if this impromptu visit to Texas is for business or pleasure?"

Sheik Omar Al Abdar flashed a slightly cool smile at the woman reporter whose voice had risen above the others. He'd only just stepped out of the private jet that had flown him from his small Middle East country of Gaspar to a private airstrip outside Mission Creek, Texas.

"I was unaware that the press had been alerted to my presence here in Texas," he replied.

"When one of the most eligible bachelors in the world comes to Texas, Texas sits up and takes notice," the reporter responded with a dazzling smile.

What if she says no? The question came unbidden to Omar's mind and he shoved it away, refusing to consider the possibility.

Rashad Aziz held up his hands to halt the volley of questions. "Please, please, His Royal Highness has traveled a long distance today and is eager to get to his final destination. He will answer no questions at this time."

"Thank you, Rashad." Omar smiled at his personal assistant once they were all settled in the car and pulling away from the circle of reporters.

Rashad smiled in welcome and withdrew a small pad from his breast pocket. "We have made arrangements for you at the Brighton Hotel in Mission Creek. The Ashbury Suite will be yours for as long as you like."

"That will be fine," Omar said absently. "And now you will tell the driver that we will go to the Carson Ranch before checking into the hotel."

Rashad didn't blink an eye. He moved to the seat directly behind the limo driver and quickly relayed the change in plans. He remained there as if instinctively recognizing Omar wanted a few moments with his own thoughts.

Omar stared out the window at the passing landscape. It irritated him that the press knew he was here. He'd hoped to fly into Mission Creek, accomplish his goal, then return to his country of Gaspar without the glare of the media upon him.

What if she says no? Again the question came from nowhere to plague him with disturbing possibility. He reached into his breast pocket and withdrew a photograph.

The picture was of a young woman in a shimmering silver ball gown. The dark-brown wavy hair that framed her heart-shaped face complemented her peaches-and-cream complexion. He remembered her eyes had been like emeralds, flirting and dancing and surrounded by thick, long lashes. A beauty mark at the corner of her mouth drew attention to the lush, thoroughly kissable-looking lips.

Elizabeth Fiona Carson. She'd been twenty-one years old when the photo had been taken at a cotillion Omar had attended in this very town. That had been six years ago and now he had come to claim her as his bride.

What if she says no?

He tucked the photo back in his pocket and straightened up in the seat. Of course she would not say no. He was Sheik Omar Al Abdar, King of Gaspar. Any woman would be proud to be chosen by him as his wife.

As the driver turned onto the Carson property, Omar once again turned his attention out the window. The Carson ranch was known for the quality of their cattle, but he was more interested in the fact that this was Elizabeth's home, the place of her birth and her upbringing.

In the letters they had exchanged over the past year, she had spoken of this place and of her parents with great affection.

As the car began to turn into the half-moon driveway in front of the house, Omar leaned forward. "No," he said. "Not the main house. There should be a caretaker's cottage somewhere on the premises." He pointed to an offshoot driveway that led past a four-car garage. "There. Go there."

The driver did his bidding, passing the garage and other outbuildings. As the car came to a halt before the little cottage, Omar felt a curious fluttering in the pit of his stomach. It couldn't be nerves, he thought. He was a sheik, the king of his country. He didn't get nervous; he made other people nervous.

Rashad opened the door to allow him to step out. With a head full of thoughts about the woman inside the cottage, Omar absently smoothed a hand down the front of his Armani suit, hoping he didn't appear too travel rumpled.

Omar drew a deep breath, aware that this moment would be one of the defining moments of his life. At thirty-eight years old, it was far past time he claimed a bride, and even though he hadn't seen Elizabeth Fiona Carson for six years, she was the woman he had chosen to make his wife.

He knocked on her door, at the same time aware of the sweet scent of the nearby flower baskets. He made a mental note to make certain there were always fresh-cut flowers in her rooms at the palace.

The door opened and Omar gazed at his bride-to-be. "Elizabeth," he said. In an instant he drank in the sight of her, pleased that she looked just as he remembered.

"Omar!" Her brilliant green eyes widened in shock at the same time her hands raced first to her hair, then to smooth down the front of her dress.

But, even though her dark wavy hair was slightly tousled and the denim dress she wore was rather plain, she looked lovely, and the desire he'd felt for her on that night so long ago sprang to life as if the six years had never passed.

"Wha-what are you doing here? I didn't know you were coming to Texas. I just got your last letter today and you didn't mention a word about coming here." She bit her bottom lip, as if aware she was rambling.

Omar found the rambling charming. He smiled at her, more certain than ever of what he was about to do. "I didn't let you know I was coming to Texas because I wanted to surprise you."

"You've certainly done that," she replied. "Uh…would you like to come in?"

"I would not be so thoughtless as to appear unannounced on your doorstep and expect you to entertain me," he replied. "I have yet to check into my hotel, but I wanted to stop here first and ask you an important question."

"Question?" She still looked stunned by his appearance, and he noticed her hand trembled slightly. "What kind of question?"

He captured her trembling hand in his, and again her beautiful green eyes widened. He could smell her fragrance, a floral scent that instantly reminded him of the night of the cotillion so long ago. "Elizabeth Fiona Carson, I have come to Texas to claim you as my wife. Will you marry me?"

* * * * *

THE COLTONS

invite you to a thrilling holiday wedding in

A Colton Family Christmas

Meet the Oklahoma Coltons—a proud, passionate clan who will risk everything for love and honor. As the two Colton dynasties reunite this Christmas, new romances are sparked by a near-tragic event!

This 3-in-1 holiday collection includes:

"The Diplomat's Daughter" by Judy Christenberry

"Take No Prisoners" by Linda Turner

"Juliet of the Night" by Carolyn Zane

And be sure to watch for **SKY FULL OF PROMISE** by Teresa Southwick this November from Silhouette Romance (#1624), the next installment in the Colton family saga.

Ring in the season with this quartet of tales that represent the true spirit of giving...*love.*

"The Ice Dancers"
by *New York Times* bestselling author
Rebecca Brandewyne

"Season of Miracles"
by Ginna Gray

"Holiday Homecoming"
by Joan Hohl

"Santa's Special Miracle"
by Ann Major

Look for these titles wherever Silhouette books are sold!

Silhouette®
Where love comes alive™

SINTMAG

Where Texas society reigns supreme—and appearances are _everything!_

Collect three (3) original proofs of purchase from the back pages of three (3) Lone Star Country Club titles and receive a free Lone Star book (regularly retailing at $4.75 U.S./$5.75 CAN.) that's not yet available in retail outlets!

Just complete the order form and send it, along with three (3) proofs of purchase from three (3) different Lone Star titles to: Lone Star Country Club, P.O. Box 9047, Buffalo, NY 14269-9047, or P.O. Box 613, Fort Erie, Ontario L2A 5X3.

LONE STAR LCC COUNTRY CLUB
EST. 1923

If you missed the first exciting stories from the Lone Star Country Club, here's a chance to order your copies today!

0-373-61352-0 STROKE OF FORTUNE
by Christine Rimmer ____ $4.75 U.S. ____ $5.75 CAN.
0-373-61353-9 TEXAS ROSE
by Marie Ferrarella ____ $4.75 U.S. ____ $5.75 CAN.
0-373-61354-7 THE REBEL'S RETURN
by Beverly Barton ____ $4.75 U.S. ____ $5.75 CAN.

(Limited quantities available.)

TOTAL AMOUNT	$_____
POSTAGE & HANDLING	$_____
($1.00 for one book, 50¢ for each additional)	
APPLICABLE TAXES*	$_____
<u>TOTAL PAYABLE</u>	$_____

(Check or money order—please do not send cash)

To order, send the completed form along with your name, address, zip or postal code, along with a check or money order for the total above, payable to Lone Star Country Club, to:

In the U.S.: 3010 Walden Avenue, P.O. Box 9047, Buffalo, NY 14269-9047; **In Canada:** P.O. Box 616, Fort Erie, Ontario L2A 5X3

Name:_____
Address:_____ City:_____
State/Prov:_____ Zip/Postal Code:_____
Account Number (if applicable):_____
093 KJH DNC 3

*New York residents remit applicable sales taxes.
*Canadian residents remit applicable GST and provincial taxes.